MANHUNT!

Mike Morrison, American adventurer, is caught in war-
torn Greece between the fleeing Allied army and the
invading German blitzkrieg. While attempting to smuggle
vital espionage papers out of the country, he becomes
the object of an intensive Gestapo manhunt—led by
deadly SS agent Konrad Heilser. In the nightmare of the
chase, Morrison shares a desperate, hopeless love with
passionate Lisa, a secret agent in the Greek underground. Inevitably, the German dragnet tightens and
Mike Morrison must break for freedom, or face certain
death. A terror-filled race through the blazing countryside provides the unforgettable climax to this classic
war-time thriller by Leon Uris.

THE ANGRY HILLS

Books by Leon Uris

BATTLE CRY
THE ANGRY HILLS
EXODUS
EXODUS REVISITED
MILA 18
ARMAGEDDON
TOPAZ
QB VII

Published by Bantam Books, Inc.

LEON URIS
THE ANGRY HILLS

BANTAM BOOKS
TORONTO · NEW YORK · LONDON

*This low-priced Bantam Book
has been completely reset in a type face
designed for easy reading, and was printed
from new plates. It contains the complete
text of the original hard-cover edition.*
NOT ONE WORD HAS BEEN OMITTED.

THE ANGRY HILLS

*A Bantam Book / published by arrangement with
Random House, Inc.*

PRINTING HISTORY

Random House edition published October 1955

Bantam edition / February 1972

2nd printing ..... March 1972	6th printing .... July 1973
3rd printing .... July 1972	7th printing .. November 1974
4th printing .... October 1972	8th printing ... February 1976
5th printing .... July 1973	9th printing ..... March 1977
	10th printing........July 1978

ISBN 0-553-12255-X

Published simultaneously in the United States and Canada

Bantam Books are published by Bantam Books, Inc. Its trade-
mark, consisting of the words "Bantam Books" and the por-
trayal of a bantam, is registered in the United States Patent
Office and in other countries. Marca Registrada. Bantam
Books, Inc., 666 Fifth Avenue, New York, New York 10019.

PRINTED IN THE UNITED STATES OF AMERICA

Many years ago I was fortunate to come into possession of a most unusual diary belonging to my uncle, Aron Yerushalmi of Tel-Aviv, Israel.

Mr. Yerushalmi had been a member of the volunteer Palestinian Brigade of the British Expeditionary Force which fought in Greece before America's entry in World War II. His extraordinary adventures took him through several captures and escapes and led him from one end of Greece to the other.

Although the characters of this book are fictitious, I was able to draw background and historical events from the diary which made this novel possible.

For *Uncle Harry*
and *Dad*

THE ANGRY HILLS

Part 1

ONE

Only five days ago the Kifissia Hotel had been almost deserted. Now it bulged with British Empire troops. In the lobby a crowd in khaki uniforms set up a steady bass hum in the variety of tongues of an international army. The uniforms were of the same drab wool but the shoulder patches told a story of the gathering of Aussies and Britons and New Zealanders and Arabs and Cyprians and Palestinians. From the bar, which stood to the right of the lobby, there came a continuous tinkle of glasses intermittently punctuated by the clang and sliding drawer of the cash register.

Over in the corner by the window, a lone civilian sat slumped in an overstuffed chair, oblivious of the hustle and bustle about him. His feet were propped on the window sill, his hat was shoved down over his eyes and an unlit pipe hung upside down from his teeth. He wore an expensive but unpressed tweed suit which looked quite in place, and his heavy wool tie was loosened at the throat. He was neither awake nor asleep—aware nor unaware—he was a study in bore-dom.

Perhaps, if you moved in literary circles or were just an avid reader of minor novels, you would recognize him on sight. Michael Morrison, an American, was one of those "bread-and-butter" writers found on every publisher's list. A writer with a small but faithful band of readers which grew slightly with each new work. The income from his four books had been augmented by regular contributions to magazines and he had written himself into a steady and comfortable income bracket of about fifteen thousand a year. It had not always been this way, to be sure. Morrison's rise was the typical writer's story of many years of struggle for acceptance, bitter disappointments and the rest of the frustrations and fears that plague that supposedly charmed profession.

A chorus of singers from the bar caused Morrison to stir. He yawned, shoved his hat back and glanced at his watch. It was still some time before his appointment. He dropped his feet from the window sill, arose and stretched and went through the business of lighting his pipe—still ignoring the assemblage of soldiers. Even at the age of thirty-five he showed traces of his earlier athletic career, for his six-foot frame carried some two hundred pounds with obvious ease. Although his face retained a little of the eternal boyish look, there were also unmistakable etchings of hardness and cynicism. In all, Michael Morrison bore a remarkable resemblance to the public's conception of a writer.

He eased his way through the crowd out to the sidewalk and stood at the curb for several moments looking for a taxi. Then he decided to walk a few squares up where the taxis were more plentiful. He was somewhat miffed at the last-minute change in accommodations forced on him which landed him in a hotel in the suburbs. All the downtown hotel space had been grabbed by the inpouring British.

As he walked, his eyes dimmed with sadness. The trip to Greece had fanned the bitter embers of memory into a flame. How often had he and his wife planned the trip! They had talked of it for years. It was to have been the honeymoon they never had. Ellie's uncle, a Greek importer, had left her a legacy of some nine thousand dollars. But each year something new arose to prevent their taking the trip. And during those years their great fear was that the money would be spent for necessary groceries instead of the purpose for which it was intended.

When at last Michael had written his way into a respectable bank balance the plans for the trip began to take real form—then exploded in an automobile accident in the fog on the Golden Gate Bridge. Ellie had been killed instantly.

It took more than a year for Morrison to find life again. There were the first months of guilt, of utter despondency, loneliness and fear of sleep because of the nightmares. Then came a period of self-pity and drink. And then the slow resurrection, with the help of his parents and many good friends but, mainly, through the love for his young son and daughter.

He would have left the money in Greece for many more years. The idea of coming to Greece without Ellie repelled him. But this was April of 1941 and the floodgates had opened. In the north, the invasion had begun. His bank and agent advised him to claim the inheritance as quickly as possible as the European situation was becoming more and more uncertain. And so, the quick trip to Athens. Morrison wanted desperately to return to San Francisco. It was no honeymoon without the bride.

"Petraki, 17," he told the cab driver and they whisked away toward Athens. Now, nearly everyone in Athens had a relative in America and this driver was no exception. In this particular case it was a brother in Cleveland. After Morrison assured the fellow that he had never been to Cleveland but would certainly look up the man's brother if he ever got there, the conversation switched to the more pressing subject of the moment.

Everything hinged, these days, on the ability of the newly arrived British Expeditionary Force to halt the German advance in the northern provinces. Only last winter the little Greek Army had run the Italians from the country, and the cab driver reasoned that if the Greeks could beat the Italians, surely the British would stop the Germans. Besides, the driver added for good measure, America would soon be in the war.

Morrison wasn't too sure of that. First, there was a big ocean, and, second, in the spring of 1941 most Americans felt there was no reason to become involved in this thing. Of course, Mike Morrison had no sympathy for Hitler. It was just, well, the type of thing the Europeans had been carrying on for centuries. It simply wasn't America's affair. He wondered about the British stopping the German advance. The Germans owned a copyright on warfare called "blitzkrieg" which had a way of crushing all opposition. And there was the undercurrent of nervous laughter all around him which seemed to imply that the British were in for a pasting.

The driver shifted his attention from politics and war to locomoting his vehicle through the congested area around Kifissia and Alexandra Streets. The traffic made him even angrier than the thought of the German Army in the north.

The shops were filled and, as in any cosmopolitan city, the citizens walked with that brisk and wonderful air of being in a hurry. But beneath the external signs of normalcy one could sense the tension, doubt and fear. British uniforms were in evidence everywhere. Young Greek males were nowhere to be seen. They were all up north or on the Albanian front. It was obvious to Mike that the enchanting Greek women were giving their British "saviors" a welcome in the best tradition. Nothing was too good for "Johnny" who had come to do combat with "Jerry" and drive him from the country.

As the cab moved south they could hear the distant wail of the air-raid sirens. The Stukas would be coming in to work over the docks at Piraeus where the B.E.F. was unloading. The British camps outside Athens were getting bombed heavily too. Morrison reckoned the Germans were kept well informed from within Athens and that the British had better get some planes in the air if they were going to make a show of it at all.

The cab came to a halt in front of the outsized yellowstone house at Petraki, 17. Morrison paid the driver and thanked him for the most interesting discussion and crossed the street.

The brass knocker beat a thunder through the ancient mansion of Fotis Stergiou. In a moment its equally ancient butler, Tassos, led him into the home of the attorney. Tassos rapped softly, then ushered him into the office of Mr. Stergiou.

The old man looked up from his all-encompassing desk and smiled a wrinkled smile of recognition. He was a quaint old duck. A shock of gray hair stood straight up from his head, a large scarf was wrapped around his shoulders and a pair of square-cut glasses were balanced precariously on the tip of his nose.

"Aha, my American writer friend, right on time, as usual," he greeted Mike and waved to a seat. "Coffee, please, Tassos," his high-pitched voice ordered. He dug through the stacks of papers on his desk and found the brief. As he opened the folder and thumbed through it, Mike once again found himself staring at the magnificent black pearl ring on the wrinkled little finger of the attorney. "Well," he finally said, "everything seems to be in good order."

"How much longer?" Mike asked.

"Always in a hurry, you Americans. One might get the idea you don't like our country."

"This is hardly the time for a leisurely visit and I do have a commitment for the first of May."

"Oh, yes, you're going to Hollywood to write a cinema—anything important?"

"Nothing but the money."

"Money—trouble is, everyone is in a grand rush to get their money out of the country these days. Can't say I blame them. The bank promised to have the final releases over here shortly for signature. When do you plan to leave?"

"I have a plane for London in the morning."

Tassos slipped in quietly.

"Coffee—good. We'll take it in the solarium, if you please, Tassos."

The two sipped coffee and exchanged tobaccos. Morrison was quite proud of his blend—a special mixture put up at Grundel's Pipe Shop in the Mission District of San Francisco. However, it was too weak for the old man. Morrison politely bowed out after a half pipeload of Stergiou's mixture.

As they passed time, Mr. Stergiou gave Morrison a short course in the Byzantine art pieces that adorned his home. As Mike had surmised, the black pearl ring was a family treasure and hadn't left his little finger for forty years.

"Your wife's death must have been quite a shock. Her uncle was truly fond of her. He spoke often of his visits to America."

"Yes—yes—it was—quite a shock."

"I see. And the children, how old are they now?"

A small smile creased the lips of the proud father and in an instant he had his wallet out and pictures thrust before the old man's nose.

Stergiou adjusted his glasses and nodded. "They are lovely children. I can well understand your anxiety to get back to San Francisco. I trust they are in good hands."

"Yes, my parents. We have a place together in Larkspur. A little over the Golden Gate Bridge from San Francisco. They—they moved in with us after Ellie's death."

The old man tapped his pipe empty in the ash tray, paused reflectively a moment, then spoke. "Mr. Morrison, I wonder if I could ask a favor of a personal nature?"

"If I can help."

"I have a document, one of great importance to a client of mine. With things so disrupted these days I am a bit hesitant to use the mails. I wonder if you would mind delivering it for me personally in London?"

"Certainly. I'd be most happy to."

The old man reached into an inside pocket of his smoking jacket and withdrew a small white envelope.

Not much of a document, Morrison thought. Stergiou held it in his hand for several seconds, then handed it to Mike. It bore a London address to one Sir Thomas Whitley.

"Normally," the old man apologized, "I wouldn't ask, but there is a great deal involved for my client and with the chaos of the day . . ."

Mike grinned. "Nothing a bit off color, by any chance?"

"Oh, you writers all have suspicious natures. No, nothing like that but a bit out of channels, if you know what I mean. I would deem it a great favor if you took extra precautions. The document does have great value."

Morrison was about to ask a question or two but decided not to. He slipped the envelope into his breast pocket. "I'll guard it with my life."

"Please do," Stergiou said, and they both laughed.

Tassos crept into the solarium and plugged a phone in beside his master. The attorney spoke briefly and replaced the receiver with a sigh. "I am terribly sorry, Mr. Morrison. They are literally swamped at the bank. It will be several hours before they will be able to get the releases over."

"I hope nothing fouls up. I do have that plane out in the morning."

"I assure you I'll stay right with it. The bank is working around the clock. Everyone is trying to get his money out of Greece these days. Could you return at—let's say eight o'clock—that will give us a safe edge in time."

"Yes, certainly."

"I apologize for the inconvenience."

Stergiou ushered Morrison down the long, statue-filled corridor and they exchanged good-byes. The instant the door closed, Stergiou spun about and shuffled quickly down the corridor and into his office. A stocky man, sporting a huge walrus mustache and bundled in an English mackintosh, sat behind Stergiou's desk. Stergiou nodded to him and filled a fresh pipe from the cannister.

"Did you give it to him?" the man asked.

Stergiou paced nervously before the desk. "Yes, I gave it to him, Major Wilken."

"Good."

"I don't like it," Stergiou said.

Major Howe-Wilken of British Intelligence arose and walked to the window and clasped his hands behind him. "Soutar and I have been under surveillance from the moment we landed in Greece. I'd wager my last quid on it. If my guess is right, Konrad Heilser is hiding out somewhere in Athens this minute directing their operation. If he is, Mr. Stergiou, our lives aren't worth a snuff."

"Then why didn't you pass the list to your military for delivery?"

"I regret to inform you that the situation at headquarters is one of utter confusion. I wouldn't wager that the military could get the King of Greece out of the country."

"In other words, Major Wilken, we are stewing in our own juice."

"Precisely. The Germans have a devilish way of gathering friends in front of their army."

Stergiou grunted and beat his fist on the desk softly. Howe-Wilken walked over to the man. "Oh, come now," he soothed, "we are not absolutely certain we've been watched. This is just an extra precaution. Soutar is out now arranging a plane to fly us out tonight. If all goes well, we should be safely in London tomorrow."

"And if all doesn't go well?"

"Then, our American friend, Mr. Morrison, will deliver the list for us. Just a precaution, mind you. Fortunately he is above suspicion."

"I don't like gambling with that list, Major. If the Germans suspect for a moment, he wouldn't have a chance—and you know the consequences of the names falling into their hands."

"Alas, my dear friend Stergiou," the major sighed, "gambling is an occupational hazard of my profession."

TWO

There were two old scores to settle and two wounds still unhealed. Konrad Heilser leaned back in the broken armchair, closed his eyes and hummed in rapid rhythm to the Bach fugue scratching out on the record player. His finger brushed down his pencil-line mustache in a motion of habit.

Howe-Wilken and his Scottish partner, Soutar, had made a fool of him twice. Eight months had passed since his first encounter with them in Norway. After the German liberation of that country, the two British agents had arrived and escaped by submarine, leaving in their wake a network of underground operators. A half dozen times he had cornered them in Norway. A half dozen times they had eluded him. It was only a damnable last-minute quirk of fate that prevented Konrad Heilser from blocking their exit from Norway.

The next time he ran into them was late last summer—Paris. Again the duo, Howe-Wilken and Soutar, led him up a blind alley while they escaped.

The German cursed softly at the thought of having been ordered from Paris to assignment in this cesspool. This time there would be a different fool. This time they would not escape.

It had been a stroke of luck, indeed, when Zervos, the government clerk, got wind of Stergiou's plan and made contact with the Germans.

Heilser slipped into Greece ahead of the German invasion and with Zervos' help got the rat pack working with him. The traitors, the opportunists, the cowards. All of them anxious to throw in with the Germans in time. Heilser and his Greek friends had done their job well. The British were confused, not knowing whom they could trust and whom not to trust. Heilser and his Greek friends had increased that confusion. The confusion that comes before defeat. Soon the confusion would be a stampeding panic.

As the record ran out Konrad Heilser stood up, flicked off the machine and lit a cigarette, the last of his pack. He walked to the mirror over the dresser and looked into it, steeped in self-admiration. He ran a brush over his already plastered-down thick black hair.

It was small wonder he felt a glow of accomplishment. No stone had been left unturned. With meticulous thoroughness he knew every move and every plan of the British. He had woven a web around them from his garret hide-away. How convenient indeed for his two old friends, Howe-Wilken and Soutar, to show up for the Stergiou list. It made everything so simple. An unexpected pleasure.

Heilser turned the record. He checked his watch, walked to the garret window and threw back the threadbare curtain. He looked down on a filthy cobblestone alley. Greece was hardly worth the conquering. A filthy, decadent race living on the past glories of two thousand years. Again, the thought of having to leave Paris angered him. If those spaghetti-eating louts of Italians hadn't been pushed from Greece and run halfway through Albania he would still be in France.

But even Greece would have its compensations. As soon as German troops liberated Athens a suite at the Grande Bretagne would be in order. Canaris, yes, even von Ribbentrop himself would hear of Heilser's splendid work. And, with the delivery of the Stergiou list, there would be a promotion. Perhaps the entire Secret Service for all of Greece would be the reward. Then, of course, there were the Greek women. This last thought made him tingle with impatience and excitement.

In the alley below, Heilser spied the figure of the fat Greek pig, Zervos, wending his way along the slime-covered cobblestones. Zervos brushed past some ragged urchins and disappeared into the house.

Heilser heard the man's footsteps grow slower and slower as he labored his way up the last flight of steps to the fifth-story attic. He could hear Zervos' wheezing breath through the flimsy door. The Greek knocked.

Zervos flopped into the armchair, fighting to regain his breath and mopping his wet face. Heilser stood over him.

"Well!" the German demanded.

"All three of them are blanketed. Howe-Wilken left by car in the direction of Stergiou's house."

"And the Scotsman, Soutar?"

"He arranges a plane to fly them from the Tatoi airdrome at midnight."

Heilser closed his eyes and put his forefinger to his forehead. He must conceal the anxious rumbling inside him from the Greek pig. He must not show anxiety before his inferior.

"The names?"

"No doubt Howe-Wilken goes to get the list now. Stergiou has contacted no one else. Tassos assures us of that."

"Good—good." The churning heightened, the coup was near at hand. . . . "And the military situation?"

"Latest information indicates the British will not make a stand before Athens."

"Then we strike!" He paced the floor rapidly. "Dispose of both Wilken and Soutar. I want Stergiou alive." He turned to Zervos. "I've waited for eight long months for this moment. . . . Watch those two; they are slippery. One mistake and I'll have your throat slit."

Zervos, the fat man, knew this wasn't idle chatter. He nodded and struggled out of the chair, still mopping his face. "One more thing disturbs me. . . . An American has visited Stergiou three times this past week."

Heilser's face reddened and a frown showed the crow's feet etched deeply in the corners of his eyes. "An American—what American?"

"We made a routine check," Zervos said. "The man is a writer—a small writer of no consequence—by name, Michael Morrison. His visa is quite in order. He is here to settle an estate. The bank bears this out. There is some nine thousand American dollars in his name. By appearances, Stergiou is doing the necessary legal work to transfer the money."

The pounding in Heilser's chest slowed. "Not getting a little jumpy—eh, Zervos?"

"Perhaps—perhaps not. We've no reason to suspect the man."

Heilser walked to the window and stared down at the alley. A mist was beginning to fall. "Go on."

"There is nothing more to say. He has a plane out for London in the morning. He stays at a hotel in Kifissia."

"Yes—yes . . ." Heilser mumbled half to himself. "It would be like Wilken and Soutar to pass off the list. A neutral above suspicion . . . Their plane at Tatoi a blind . . ."

The record ended.

Heilser shut off the machine, picked up the record and began to toy with it. Then he placed it gently on the dresser and stood frozen. The cigarette between his fingers burned down until he felt its heat on his fingers. He opened his fingers and watched the burning butt fall to the floor. With the ball of his foot he squashed the butt, then ground it into powder.

THREE

Morrison was completely unaware of the tall thin blond man wearing a New Zealand uniform who picked up his trail the instant he left the attorney's mansion. Nor was he aware of the half dozen pairs of eyes focused upon the house from points of observation nearby. Mike walked through the plush Kolonaki sector toward Concord Square across town, drawing his topcoat about his neck against the mist.

Concord Square was filled with the usual mid-afternoon crowd either scurrying to and from the sub-way or settled in the many coffee houses to argue the day away. The flower stalls were a blaze of color that helped offset the drizzly overcast.

He stopped to find his bearings and immediately fell prey to one of those sidewalk shoeshine hustlers who have the knack of spotting an American a mile away. The tall blond man in New Zealand uniform took up his vigil from a sidewalk table at one of the coffee houses.

The earlier undercurrent of tension was more perceptible, Morrison thought. Although the chatter was foreign, he could still deduce from snatches of conversation around him that the British were going to withdraw from Athens. People walked as if in a stupor and their faces betrayed a mixture of fear and confusion and disbelief.

A flood of uneasiness hit Mike. He counted the long hours ahead till dawn when he would be winging toward London. The shoeshine boy applied the final touches with a pair of oversized brushes and stepped back to admire his work. Americans' shoes always shined so well. He received a handsome tip. For several moments Mike stood and looked in all directions contemplating the best way to kill the afternoon. The National Museum was closed and its treasures removed. He looked down Athena Street to its end and saw the rise of the Acropolis. No, he did not want to go there again. Rather silly, not wanting to sightsee, but his few side trips had left him depressed, for Ellie was not there. She would never see them. For a moment he considered the idea of the American Bar but visualized an afternoon's dull conversation with a visiting fireman. He was hungry but ruled out trying another strange restaurant. Yesterday he had found a place in Cavouri, twenty miles from Athens overlooking a picturesque bay, but he could still taste the olive oil.

He began tō wander, hands in pockets, along Aeoluš Street where the conglomeration of food in the sidewalk stalls sent up a sickening odor. The shoppers and stallkeepers haggled, but the performance was half-hearted today. Their thoughts were on tomorrow. He window-shopped and remembered the thousand hours he window-shopped with Ellie when they could afford no other pastime. He purchased two pairs of peasant slippers with bright red pompons on the toes for Jay and Lynn and strolled on.

The next intersection brought an onrush of British troops from the camp at Kokinia. Then Morrison's eye caught a sign he could read in any language.

The saloon was half-empty and the stock at rock bottom. A choice of two types of *krasi*. He stood at the far end of the bar, and after the first sip was thankful his long tenure as an unpublished writer hadn't given him the opportunity to cultivate a taste for fine liquors. The tall blond man in the New Zealand uniform entered and sat near the door.

A half bottle later, much of the tension had eased inside Mike. As the bar filled with soldiers he made an honorable retreat to a table with his bottle. He observed and he drank.

The soldiers of the British Expeditionary Force were on the edge of collapsing morale. Morrison heard bitter complaints about the bombings of the camps and the lack of combat units in the force. The colonials, in soldiers' jargon, had a word or two to say about the support they were receiving.

About three-quarters of the way through the bottle of *krasi*, the noise in the place seemed to fade. He banished his rambling thoughts about his children, whom he missed terribly, and quickly diverted his mind to guessing what was in the envelope and what kind of shady deal Mr. Stergiou was mixed up in. He overcame the temptation to open the envelope for a quick peek and instead wove a half dozen different plots about its contents. Morrison's one attempt at mystery writing ended. He gave up.

"Mind if I sit down?"

Mike looked up into the face of the tall blond man in New Zealand uniform. He glanced toward the bar; it was three deep. He nodded to the man.

"Bit crowded there ... Mosley's the name, Jack Mosley—First New Zealand Rifles." The lance corporal began to open his bottle.

"Might as well finish this one first," Mike said, pouring.

Mosley pulled out a pipe. Pipe smokers have a common bond. "Here, try some good stuff," Mike said, flipping his pouch over the table. Mosley loaded, lit, drew and approved.

"You're an American, aren't you?"

Mike balked. The answer often led to an argument. "Yes, I'm an American."

"Goodo. I like Americans. What the devil are you doing in Greece these days?"

Mike's tongue loosened as they started on Mosley's bottle of *krasi*. As it emptied and another bottle came he gave the entire story, complete with pictures of Jay and Lynn. Mosley returned the compliment, showing pictures of three of his own. Mike found his drinking partner friendly and intelligent and, as the wine struck home, his talk turned to an outpouring.

The saloon was smoky now with a blend of powerful Turkish and flat-smelling British tobaccos. Singers were deep in harmony, forgetting, for the moment, their troubles. Streetwalkers wandered in and couples left.

"And what line of business are you in, Morrison?"

It was a question he dreaded. When a person meets a writer there is an expectant glow, as though he had run into Hemingway or Faulkner. It always embarrasses the non-professional when he has never heard of the writer.

"Morrison—of course, forgive me," Mosley said. "I enjoyed *Home Is the Hunter* very much—splendid book."

"Really! Well, have another glass of wine, my friend."

"Tell me, Morrison. Are you really as bitter about life as your book indicates?"

Mike was used to it. With the purchase of a book the buyer automatically gets a critic's license. Not that he minded much. It was the ones who borrowed a book and became critics who annoyed him. However, he was surprised to find Mosley's comments extremely sharp as well as objective. The wine was good and the noise was loud and he bought another bottle.

Mike covered a great deal of ground, from literature to wars to San Francisco to Greece to music. In fact, there was very little he didn't cover. The subjects began to overtake one another, then run into one another. He more than made up for the four days of sulking quiet in Greece. Mike was entirely too talky and heady to realize or care that his companion was barely drinking at all.

Then, as all such converstations generally do, it swung around to the subject of women and sex.

"Mosley, feel I know you well enough to pose a ver' serious question. . . . Question is, are you one of those fellows completely faithful to your spouse?"

"Only on occasion," Mosley answered.

"Well, this isn't the occasion. Tell you what we're gonna do—tell you what. We're gonna wheel and deal over to Constitution Square to one of those plush joints and pick us up a pair of ladies. . . ."

"Corking idea."

"They don't hardly make guys like you any more Mosley. . . . No, sir . . . You're O.K. in my book. . . ."

Mike struggled to his feet and promptly slumped to his chair. He emitted a long, long whistle. "Stuff gangs up on you . . ." He whistled again. "Stuff's loaded."

This time, with Mosley's aid, he managed to get to a vertical position. The man in the New Zealand uniform guided him through the crowd onto the sidewalk. The night air almost flattened him.

"Hey, wait a minute, wait a minute, wait a minute, read my watch . . . whatsit say?"

"Half-past eight."

"Hell—I forgot—I got a 'pointment . . . Look, tell you what we're gonna do . . . You go over to the Kifff—the Kiffff—the goddamn Kiffffisssssia Hotel and wait in my room . . . Got this 'pointment . . . Hotel sits on the side of the mountain—over thataway . . . Soon's I get back from my 'pointment you an me are going to get fixed up—know what I mean?"

Mosley spilled Morrison into a cab and waved as Mike poked his head out of the window. "Kiffffisssssia— thataway—they don't make them like you any more. . . ."

As Mike's cab turned the corner, an automobile U-turned and stopped at the curb where Mosley waited. He opened the door and hopped in.

"Shall we follow him?" the driver asked.

"No—we'll rejoin Zervos."

"What about the American?"

Mosley smiled and stretched back. "Let the fool go. If he is a British agent, I'm Winston Churchill."

FOUR

Mike stood opposite the yellow-stone mansion at Petraki, 17. The street was black and empty. He wavered back and forth and made an abortive attempt to light his pipe. He mumbled drunkenly to himself, staggered across the street and managed to negotiate the opposite curb. He swayed up the steps and reached for the big brass knocker. It hit the plate and the door jarred open.

He leaned against the door frame, bracing himself and waiting for Tassos to come. He pulled the knocker again—waited—waited—nothing.

"Only got one good ear between them anyhow . . ."

Mike shoved the door and plunged into a pitch-black hallway. He fumbled through his pockets, found his matches and lit one and squinted around. The match burned his fingers. He dropped it and yelled out an oath. He lit another and found the hall switch.

The hallway lit up. It was long and dimly lit and lined with white marble statues.

"Stergiou! Wake up!" His echo bounced through the place weirdly.

He staggered farther into the hall and called again. The house was eerie and his head reeled from the wine.

"Stergiou, come out, come out, wherever you are!"

He bumped into a statue and it swayed on its pedestal. Mike draped his arms around it to keep it from falling and bowed and apologized. "Stergiou!"

He stood before the door to the old man's office.

"Probably sleep at his desk—probably—probably is ..."

Mike leaned against the door and pitched into the office. The door groaned shut behind him. His hands groped for the light switch. He hit a chair and smashed to the floor with it. He lay there, unable to lift himself, hit with sudden spinning dizziness. ...

He struggled to his hands and knees and began to crawl. The journey stopped as his head cracked against the desk. Mike reached his hand to the desk top and he grunted as he rose to his feet and felt around the desk for a lamp.

The lamplight broke the room into dim yellow and black shadows. He propped himself against the desk and shook his head to clear the alcoholic fog. His eyes peered into the shadows and he scanned the room. It was a shambles!

A sound.

He reached to switch off the light, then froze.

There—on the floor—Stergiou's glasses—smashed, and the carpet red with blood around them.

"Morrison," a voice whispered from the shadow.

The blood rushed from Mike's lips as a jolt of fear hit him. His throat muscles tightened into dryness ...

"Morrison," the voice whispered again.

Mike's jaw trembled open. "Who are you?" he croaked unevenly.

"Over—by the door," the voice said.

"Who are you? Where is Stergiou?"

"Stergiou's dead."

Morrison's breath came in short frightened grunts. He shook his head again. It was a nightmare! A nightmare like the ones he had when Ellie died. His head turned slowly and he strained his eyes ... Yes, there was someone there. . . . Through the dull yellow shadow he could see a man's face staring at him.

"No—no—no—no . . . Leave me alone—leave me alone . . . I'm—I'm getting out of here. . . ." He lurched toward the door in blind fear.

"Morrison! Stand still! I have a gun on you!"

The command halted him.

Mike's eyes bulged in terror. His face was wet with sweat. He looked at the man. The man sat in a chair. . . . There were streaks of blood running from the corners of the man's mouth and the man's big walrus mustache was red with blood.

"What do you want of me?" Mike pleaded. "What have I done?"

"The envelope—the envelope—you must deliver it . . . A plane—leaves Tatoi airdrome—midnight—take my credentials . . ."

Mike's hands fumbled through his pockets. He found the envelope. "Take the damned thing—take it . . . I'm an American citizen—you've no right to mix me up in this . . ."

The man groaned and his eyes rolled and on his face appeared the stamp of death. His whisper fluttered. . . . "You have no choice, Morrison. They'll get you. . . . They are on to you. . . . Don't—don't try the American Embassy. . . . They'll have it surrounded. . . . They—they have friends—everywhere. . . . You—have no choice, Morrison."

The hand holding the pistol dropped limply and the pistol clattered to the floor. Mike grabbed the man's lapel.

"Who are *they?*" he said. "Who are *they?*"

The man's head rolled back. His lips trembled open but he was unable to speak. Mike bent down and picked up the pistol and put the credential card in his pocket.

The man groaned. Mike blinked from the sting of the salt from the sweat in his eyes as he backed off toward the door and stepped into the hallway.

FIVE

Morrison bolted down the hallway and through the door. He stopped abruptly on the doorstep and looked right and left in desperation.

Petraki Street was as still as a morgue. The drizzle put a shiny coat on the pavement in the glow of the lamplights.

He walked as quickly as his wobbly legs could bear him toward the Avenue Vasilissis Sofias. The Avenue would be filled with people—he must reach it quickly. The still of the night was broken only by the sound of his heels beating against the sidewalk.

He stopped short.

From behind came the sound of a motor starting—slow acceleration—the noise of wet tires rolling. Morrison fell back into the shadows and flattened himself against a wall. A black car, headlights out, inched toward him. Mike closed his eyes and swayed, on the verge of blacking out. He gritted his teeth to muffle the sound of his breathing. A moment passed. The car halted at the intersection, then turned into Ravine Street. The sound of the motor faded.

Mike began to run full speed down the glassy street.

He stumbled on the curb, struggled up and ran again, his heart nearly tearing through his chest. He saw the Avenue ahead of him—and stopped in terror.

"Oh, God, no!"

The Avenue Vasilissis Sofias was devoid of life. The wide boulevard had not a car—not a sign of a human on it. The houses were dark—no light shone except for a dim street lamp.

Let me wake up! Let me wake up! he cried to himself. He continued running down the deserted thoroughfare—two blocks—three—four—until everything blurred.

He stopped. He was facing the square white marble of the Byzantine Museum. He was unable to take another step. A whining sang through his ears. . . .

There! Down the street—a light. Morrison staggered down the Avenue and edged toward the light. He peered through the window. The saloon was empty except for the barkeep.

Mike buckled over the bar, panting for breath. The bartender stared at him wide-eyed. "English," Mike gasped. "You speak Englezos?"

The bartender began rambling in Greek.

"Englezos—telephone—ring—ring . . ."

Mike fished through his pocket and slapped a bill on the counter. He stumbled back of the bar to the phone. The bartender glanced at the money and kept his confused vigil.

"Operator—operator—hello . . . Can you understand me . . . Englezos? Thank God . . . American Embassy . . . No—no—American Embassy . . . That's right, that's right—hurry—please . . ."

Mike closed his eyes and whispered under his breath as he heard a ring—then two, three, four. "Answer, dammit, answer! Eight—nine—ten—eleven . . ."

He slid the phone back on the hook and leaned against the back of the bar trying to think through the fog. A sob broke through his lips and tears rolled from his eyes. . . .

"Operator," he said softly, "operator . . . Englezos."

The operator did not understand. He held the phone a moment.

"Operator," he whispered. "Englezos, yes, Englezos . . . I want Associated Press . . . Associated Press. American News. Yes, that's right . . ."

Ring—ring.

"A.P., Watson speaking."

"Mister—mister—I'm an American. . . . I'm in trouble."

"You'd better call the Embassy then."

"No, wait! Don't hang up. They didn't answer. . . . You've got to help me."

"Go on."

"They're after me—they're trying to kill me."

"What is this, a gag?"

"No—no . . . I tell you they're trying to kill me."

"Go on, Fred. Stop trying to disguise your voice—we're busy now."

"For God's sake! Listen to me!"

"Hey, is this on the level?"

"Yes—yes—on the level . . ."

"Say, you sound drunk to me."

"I'm drunk. . . . I can't help it. . . . They're after me. . . . You've got to help me."

"Who's after you?"

"I don't know . . ."

The line went dead. Mike clicked it a dozen times. "Hello . . . hello . . . hello . . ."

He froze against the back of the bar as he saw the black automobile cruise slowly in front of the saloon.

Outside, he hugged the shadows praying for his head to clear—praying for a sign of human life. A block away he came to the National Gardens. The trees and shubbery and blacked-out lanes would give him cover for the moment. The trees dripped moisture under the gentle rustle of a small wind. Each new sound startled him. His brain reeled in confusion.

Morrison circled about aimlessly, keeping off the paths, clinging to the high hedges. A large building loomed ahead of him. Parliament Building, he thought ... Constitution Square was near.

"There must be someone ... There must be people ..."

The Avenue Amalia opened before him and the Square beyond it. The Square was empty—the street deserted. He knelt in the brush for several moments. A taxi stopped before the Tomb of the Unknown Soldier.

Morrison dashed forward, flung the back door open and fell into the seat.

"Everyone—where has everyone gone?"

"The British are withdrawing from Athens. The people stay in their homes. ... Where do you wish to go?"

"Go? Take me—take me—just drive."

It was so horribly strange—all of it was so horribly strange. If his head would only clear—if he could only think. His hand felt something in his pocket. He looked at the credential: MAJOR THEODORE HOWE-WILKEN: INTELLIGENCE SERVICE. The small white envelope was in his hand. ...

"Take me—take me to the Tatoi Airdrome."

SIX

The taxi sped through the slippery streets, jolting to sudden stops and taking turns on two wheels with a total disregard for life and limb.

The waves of fear slowly subsided in Morrison, but the events of the past hours were as blurred as the buildings he sped past. It was still impossible for him to think clearly. He knew he must not close his eyes for he would pass out. He clung to one thought as he fought off the walls of unconsciousness closing in on him. He had to get on that airplane at Tatoi and get as far away from Athens and Greece as he could. It was only this basic instinct of self-preservation that held back the effects of three bottles of *krasi* and the lightning chain of events that had followed.

At ten forty-five the taxi screeched to a halt before an entanglement of barbed wire which encompassed the air field.

"Put out those headlights," a sentry ordered.

Mike reeled from the cab, paid the driver and staggered toward the sentry.

"There's a plane for me. . . . Major—Major Howe-Wilken."

The guard studied the wavering figure with much apprehension. Morrison was, indeed, a very sorry sight.

"May I see your pass?"

"Pass . . . Sure—sure . . ."

The soldier took the card and stepped into the small

guard shack and turned a muffled flashlight on it. He returned to Mike, snapped to attention and peeled off a rigid British salute to perfection. Mike sighed in relief.

The guard went into the shack again and cranked the phone. "This is Private Edmonds, station three. Major Howe-Wilken has arrived. Yes, sir, very good, sir." He hung up.

"Won't you step in, Major? A command car will be here for you in a few moments. That's your plane over there, sir, on the east runway."

Much of the overcast had broken. A few stars peeked down and a quarter moon played hide and seek behind the scattering clouds. Mike squinted through the window. Far across the field he made out the shadowed outline of a large transport.

He found his pipe and patted his pockets for matches.

"Sorry, sir, but I'll have to ask that you refrain from smoking. Blackout regulations, you know."

" 'Scuse me . . ."

There was a great to-do outside. The air was filled with the sound of motors. Mike walked to the door and looked to the nearby highway. A long convoy of trucks filled with soldiers ground to a halt.

"What's all that?"

"Troops from the Camp at Kokinia, sir. They're stopping to pick up our detachment at the airport, sir. Bloody shame, if you ask me, Major, about us pulling out of Athens. We'd give the Hun a show if they let us. Oh, forgive me, Major Wilken, but there were some inquiries for you."

Mike spun around from the door.

"Chap in a New Zealand uniform—a lance corporal —didn't give his name. He was with a rather fat gentleman. Greek, I'd suppose. He asked if you'd checked through."

Mike again felt the clammy cold of fear. . . .

"And the other chap drove by just a few moments ago. Mr. Soutar."

"Soutar?"

"Yes, sir. Little thin bloke with horn-rimmed specs. Scotsman, if I've ever heard one."

Mike's fist tightened around the pistol in his pocket. He looked through the night to the plane. He could hear the first spitting sounds of its motor turning over to warm up.

Get on it . . . I'll get on it. . . . I'll get on it. . . .

"What the hell's keeping that car?"

"Sorry, sir, it should be here shortly."

Private Edmonds watched, puzzled, from a respectful distance as Mike began a nervous, wavering pacing. The private listened as Mike's breathing turned to labored grunts. He looked into Mike's bleary eyes. . . . Strange ducks, these Intelligence chaps, Private Edmonds thought.

An automobile raced over the east runway. It halted two hundred yards away as a chorus of air-raid sirens screamed around the field.

A distant sound of approaching motors from the invisible sky above.

The occupants of the car scattered on the runway.

The sound of the motors above turned to a drone and became louder and louder.

A shattering roar as anti-aircraft batteries split the air and white puffs of smoke exploded in the sky after a crisscross of pencil-slim lights darted and probed.

The overhead motors were suddenly silent.

For the first time, Mike Morrison heard that hideous scream—the scream of Stukas.

To the sirens and the whistles below, the Stukas answered with a discordant symphony of their own.

Men fled from the convoy at the roadside amid desperate, aimless commands.

The shriek of the Stukas became louder as they swooped like vultures on their prey.

The earth danced amid blinding flashes of light and fearful ear-bursting blasts.

Mike dropped to the floor and covered his ears. The scream tore across the field again. His hands tried to claw through the wooden floor. The shack bounced and Mike saw the dazed guard career into a wall and roll to the floor unconscious.

Mike crawled to the door and shoved it open. The airdrome was a field of bright orange flames reaching toward the sky. In its light he saw the airplane on the east burn into searing oblivion.

A plan of desperation hit him. He crawled back to the prostrate body of the guard. The scream again! A blast rolled him against the wall. They won't get me! They won't get me!

He half tore the clothes from the guard's body. . . . They won't get me . . . they won't get me . . . He tugged at the man's pants; then ripped his own clothes from him.

He struggled into the guard's clothes as the thunder outside rose to a crescendo.

His hands fished through the pockets of his own clothes. Envelope—wallet—pipes—passport—the credential—pistol . . .

He staggered through the doorway.

A shadow raced over the runway toward the shack. "Morrison! Morrison!" a voice pierced through the inferno. "Morrison! Morrison! Morrison!" The shadow took the form of a man.

Mike stumbled, crawled, bolted toward the line of trucks on the highway.

Then everything was quiet.

The planes vanished and the air was still.

The lights around the field blinked off leaving only the glow of the fire.

Mike knelt beside a truck, clutched at his stomach then rolled over on the ground. "Oh, Jesus—Jesus—I'm sick—I'm sick . . ."

The spinning would not stop. American Embassy—they'll get you—they'll get you—empty wet streets—oh, go on Fred, we're busy—no time for gags—they'll get you—they'll get you—blood trickled from the corner of his mouth and his mustache was wet with blood—the glasses lay smashed—long hall with white marble statues—Kifissia Hotel, thataway . . .

Then there was nothing.

"Bloody Huns!"

"Hey, Tom. Over here. I think this bloke's been hit."

"From the smell of him I'd say he's been on too much Greek wine."

"All right, lads, hop to it. Get aboard the lorries."

"Give us a hand, sergeant. He's out cold."

Mike's body was shoved aboard the truck. The tail gate clanged shut behind him.

The convoy roared off.

SEVEN

Morrison looked through a window. On the other side of the window faces stared at him—a hundred faces and the faces stared at him with shocked eyes. The faces wore masks of terror. Faces of Greeks.

The window began to move and the faces blurred.

Mike bolted up in his seat then slid back. His head pounded and throbbed. There was a dry, pasty, miserable taste in his mouth and a queasy feeling in his stomach. He grunted and rubbed his temples.

On the opposite seat Mike saw a man stretched out. He was in uniform and his face was wrapped in bandages. The man groaned.

Mike pushed out of his seat and stretched. He was in a compartment on a train. He looked down the aisle and saw other compartments filled with wounded soldiers.

He flopped into his seat and dropped his head into his hands. Then, the first of the recollections came to him. A voice in the shadows, "you have no choice, Morrison. . . ."

Mike fumbled wildly through his pockets. He held the card—MAJOR THEODORE HOWE-WILKEN: INTELLIGENCE . . . He stared at the small white envelope . . .

The train clickety-clacked past a grove of olive trees. The soldier opposite him moaned again and rolled and twisted in agony.

Mike sat through several moments of puzzled

silence. Snatches of memory returned and he began to fit pieces together. So many of the events seemed hazy; others he could not recall. He looked about him again. The train—the uniform—the envelope—the pass. It was no nightmare—it had really happened.

He found the comfort of his pipe and tried to reason the situation out. Stergiou, the attorney, was obviously mixed up in something of importance. The "something" being the contents of the small white envelope. An adversary wanted the envelope. . . . British Intelligence was in on it, so, Mike reasoned, the Germans were the adversaries.

He shuddered as he reviewed the harrowing hours. "I'll be damned," he muttered.

Michael Morrison knew as much as he wanted to know. One thing was certain: he was going to get out of the whole affair quickly.

The fright of yesterday turned to anger. The audacity of that Stergiou!

He rubbed his temples again and the throbbing eased. Then he laughed to himself. "Damnedest thing, they'll never believe me when I tell them about this at the Press Club—damnedest thing."

The train stopped.

There was a sound of digging outside.

The door of the compartment opened. A man wearing the Red Cross arm band of a medic entered.

After examining the wounded soldier opposite Mike, the medic opened his kit and pumped a shot of morphine into the man's arm. "Easy now, chappie, the doctor will be by shortly." The medic turned to Mike. "I see you're up now. How are you feeling?"

"Little the worse for wear."

"We examined you when they put you aboard last night. Couldn't locate a wound. If you're feeling better

you'd best rejoin your unit. You'll find them somewhere about on the train."

"What's going on out there?" Mike asked.

"We've reached Corinth—taking on another detachment of troops."

"What's the digging?"

"Sappers. They're going to blow the bridges after the
last of the trains pass. We're withdrawing into lower
Greece, the Peloponnesus."

Mike felt his heart sink. He had to make a move
quickly.

"I say. You'd better get back to your unit."

"Who's in command of the train?" Mike asked curtly.

"Colonel Potter—why?"

Mike flashed Major Howe-Wilken's card at the medic. "Find the Colonel and tell him I wish to speak to
him immediately."

"Yes, sir." The medic retreated to the door.

"Soldier!"

"Yes, Major."

"Not a word to anyone but Colonel Potter."

"Yes, sir."

The medic left.

The rest would be quite simple, Mike thought. He'd
explain the entire story to Colonel Potter. He had the
papers and his own passport to authenticate everything.
It was, after all, British responsibility. They would be
obligated to escort him back to Athens or arrange a
flight out.

Several moments passed. Mike stared out of the window and watched the new troops board. Poor devils, he
thought. At least he'd be out of Greece soon. . . .

As the last unit boarded the train one of the men
attracted his attention. He didn't know why, but Mike

found himself staring at a short man wearing large horn-rimmed glasses. Perhaps he looked so much out of place in the company of soldiers. The man couldn't have been much over five feet tall and his uniform literally hung on him. Another peculiarity—the little man carried none of the paraphernalia of soldiers. There was only an outsized pistol strapped to his waist. He certainly seemed no part of an army. Mike's curiosity gave way to uneasiness.

Something about him—something about him ... What was it? Yes ... Yes, he was standing in the guard shack at the airdrome. The sentry said something, something about a man who was looking for him. A little man with horn-rimmed glasses. The sentry had given a name but Mike couldn't remember it.

The little man boarded the train.

Mike tried to reason with himself. He was still jumpy, that's all. No—no—he wasn't jumpy. Stergiou's office—the voice that spoke to him from the shadows ... The man with the walrus mustache, Howe-Wilken, his voice had whispered, "They have friends, everywhere. . . . They'll get you, Morrison."

The train jerked into motion.

The door opened. Mike looked up with a start. It was the medic.

"Major Howe-Wilken."

"Yes."

"Colonel Potter will see you, sir. The Colonel is in the fourth car forward, third compartment."

Mike stumbled into the aisle as the train lurched around a bend. He hung onto the hand rail and moved down the car past the compartments of wounded soldiers. One thought: get off the train—get off it!

He reached the end of the car and pulled at the door. It was stuck tight. He tugged hard again and it opened. A blast of air greeted him as he stepped onto the platform. He gripped the rail and braced himself to jump. The ground tore past him with terrifying speed. No, it would be suicide.

Mike looked about. Maybe—maybe, with luck, he could reach Colonel Potter.

He stepped forward to the next platform and peered through the door window. The car had no compartments. It was jammed with soldiers. Good luck.

Mike opened the door and looked about cautiously. He scanned every face in the car as he moved ahead slowly, stepping over the packs and rifles that blocked the aisle.

End of the car.

He crossed the platform to the next car. Palestinians. Down the aisle he worked, then crossed to the next car.

Colonel Potter was in the next car up. Mike was coming closer and closer to his deliverance.

He stopped dead in his tracks. Leaning against the door, blocking it, stood a man. The man's icy blue eyes were on Mike. He was tall and blond and wore a New Zealand uniform. The man in the bar who called himself Jack Mosley.

Mike felt for the pistol. It was gone!

The two glared at one another. Mosley dropped his cigarette, stepped on it and moved toward Mike.

Morrison spun about and shot through the car, onto the platform and through the carload of Palestinians.

Through the next car—and the next.

When he reached the jammed door of his own car he forced his shoulder against it until it finally burst open.

He halted his flight midway up the aisle. The door to his compartment was open. In the reflection of the glass he could see the little man with horn-rimmed glasses.

"You say he was here!"

"Yes, sir," Mike heard the medic answer.

"Where did he go?"

"Forward, sir, to Colonel Potter—three cars down."

"I've got to reach him first."

Mike ducked into a compartment where two wounded soldiers lay. The little man in the horn-rimmed glasses rushed past.

Mike jumped out into the aisle and began to race back. "They'll get you, Morrison. They'll get you. . . . They'll get you. . . ."

He reached the rear platform—the end of the train. A blur of olive trees, and the ribbons of steel shooting out under the wheels and disappearing on the horizon.

Mike looked through the glass. The tall New Zealander was entering the opposite end of the car. There was a pistol in his hand. He walked slowly, looking into each compartment. He raised his eyes toward the rear platform, raised the pistol and made for it.

EIGHT

Clickety clack—clickety clack—clickety clack . . .

Michael Morrison balanced himself on the edge of the step. The ground tore past him.

Clickety clack—clickety clack—clickety clack . . .

He eased back to the platform and crouched beside the door, poised to spring on Mosley the instant the door opened.

The train screeched to a sudden stop and Mike's feet flew out from under him.

The sound from the sky—he knew it now—Stukas!

Little black specks circled overhead and began to take form as they dropped lower.

Mike leaped from the platform and rolled down the siding. Behind him men poured from the train, from the platform, through the windows . . .

The motors in the sky were suddenly still. A second passed—two—three . . .

The scream—the hideous scream as the bombs fell to earth. Mike covered his head. . . . The ground rumbled and split under the impact of the bombardment.

The first volley fell wide of the train. Everyone was up and running madly over the field toward a grove of olive trees. They fell and clawed at the earth as the Stukas came in for a second pass.

Over his shoulder Mike saw the third car disintegrate. The line of cars went into a snake dance. The engine skittered off the track and rolled down the rail bed, snorting and hissing.

Mike tumbled in at the edge of the olive grove. Soldiers poured in all about him and fell flat and lay motionless.

The Stukas turned from the destroyed train and began to blast the soldiers in the field who were scurrying like frightened ants. The planes cut them down like blades of grass then roared in on the olive grove at tree-top level. Their wings spit little gusts of fire and the trees whined and ricocheted bullets. A soldier shrieked, then lay very still.

"Here they come again!"

"Bloody bastards!"

They swept in so low that Mike could make out the face of one of the pilots. A soldier near him kneeled

and fired his rifle defiantly. He shook his fist and
screamed an oath. An officer ran to the soldier and
jerked the rifle from his hand.

"You damned fool! Do you want them to know
where we are?" the officer yelled.

"God dammit! They know where we are! What kind
of a war is this . . . ?"

The argument ended as a hail of bullets ripped the
earth around them.

On and on, wave after wave worked over the grove
without mercy or respite. Ten minutes, twenty minutes,
thirty minutes . . . Streaking tracers, thundering motors
. . .

Then, their bombs gone, their machine guns empty,
the Stukas ended their sport and flew off.

It was deathly silent in the grove. The men were too
stunned to budge. Mike sat up and dropped his head
on his knees. "Holy Mother of God," he whispered as
the last motor faded from hearing.

After a while a slow movement started. Soldiers
walked in dazed circles and spoke in shaky whispers. In
another five minutes the grove was a bedlam of men
running and shouting.

Someone tapped Mike on his shoulder.

A young Australian captain stood over him. "You
there, get over there." He pointed to a unit of men
forming outside the grove.

Mike wobbled to his feet. "Colonel Potter—where is
he?"

"The Colonel's been hit," the captain said.

"I want to speak to the next in command." He dug
into his pockets for the credential. It was missing. Mike
looked about. Some soldiers were staring at him. The
whole place was in utter confusion. It would be useless
. . .

"Sorry, sir," Mike said to the captain and he joined the group of men at the edge of the grove.

Other officers were forming groups of a hundred men, regardless of former units. The Aussie captain stood before Mike's group.

"All right, lads, pay attention," the captain said. "With those Stukas about, we've got to stay in small units. No more train rides . . ."

Feeble laughter.

"We strike out by foot and stay together."

"Captain, sir, where are we going?"

"That's a top secret," the captain lied. He wished he knew.

"If the Stukas come again, sir, may we fire back?"

It was a ridiculous question. There were but twelve Enfields in the group of a hundred men. Many more ridiculous questions were asked about water and rations. The captain seemed short on answers.

They moved out over the rails toward the foothills, marching at a murderous pace in search of refuge before the Stukas returned.

As for Michael Morrison, American tourist . . . He was helplessly snarled in a gang of desperate, fleeing men. It was useless for him to try to find someone in command—no one seemed to be in command. Where to go? What to do? Where to run? Where to hide?

As the afternoon wore on, Mike began to limp from the nonstop hike. He remembered feeling like this once before in his life. Those first weeks after Ellie's death he had gone through the outward motions of living, but everything inside him had dried up and his mind had been clouded by fear and hopelessness.

The column pressed deeper and deeper into the foothills. The soldiers were weary beyond words—too weary even to gripe. The terrain became more rugged as they pushed on. When the sun dropped behind the far hills and the air had cooled, the captain decided it would be safe to take a break.

The men scattered among the rocks and brush after guzzling at a stream, despite warnings from the NCO's.

Darkness fell on the Peloponnesus . . .

The soldiers fell into fitful exhausted sleep.

But Michael Morrison dared not indulge in the luxury. Through bloodshot eyes he kept vigil during the black hours. A vigil against the little man in the horn-rimmed glasses and the tall blond man who called himself Jack Mosley. Who were they? How many others were looking for him? Everyone was to be eyed with suspicion—everyone!

Mike dozed fitfully, but every whisper of a tree, every stir of a restless sleeper brought him fully awake. He mumbled to himself, snatches of poems, dialogues from his books, anything to keep himself awake. . . .

Dawn.

The second day the group wandered aimlessly, deeper and deeper into the hills, making for the mountains.

The Stukas came and found them. The turkey shoot was on again. Seven times during the day the group was sighted and seven times they flung themselves to earth. . . . And each time they arose and reeled about like punch-drunk fighters and pushed on.

The unholy rape of Greece was on. Every village along the march of the retreating British Expeditionary Force was leveled to the ground.

There was no relief. The vultures in the sky hovered over them and dogged their every step. At last the young Aussie captain gave the order to halt for the day. They would move by night.

Mike kept his agonized vigil until sunset. They might

be lurking behind every rock, every tree, waiting to pounce on him.

He stumbled on through the long black night. Each time he fell a nameless soldier would pull him to his feet and offer a word of encouragement. In the hours before dawn two soldiers half-dragged, half-carried him along the tortuous route.

The third day found them cowering in a lemon grove near a village, sweating out the daylight hours.

A wonderful daze enveloped Mike. He could see and he could hear but sounds seemed to come from a great distance. He could touch but he was numb to feeling. He could walk without falling but had no sense of movement. He could speak but his words were inaudible to him.

While the unit lay asleep, exhausted from the night's march, Mike sat propped against a tree, his eyes wide open.

He cocked his head and looked down the rows of lemon trees. Sunlight filtering through the tree tops created weird shadows and the shadows flickered under a soft breeze.

A sudden glint at the edge of the grove some three hundred yards away caught his attention. Mike blinked. A reflection from some type of glass ... Then he saw the outline of a man. The glint again—the man's glasses. The figure walked slowly between two rows of trees, half in shadow, half in dancing sunlight. ... A small man—a very small man—and he walked through the shadows toward the group of sleeping soldiers.

NINE

"Where the devil do you think you're going?" the Aussie captain said.

"Water," Mike rasped. "I need water. Village . . ."

The captain was about to order him back to the grove. He studied Morrison. The bloke was in wretched condition . . . worse off than the rest of his troops. He carried no rations or canteen. Perhaps it would be better to let him get some food and water and freshen up. Otherwise they may have to be packing him and he'd slow the whole group down.

"Very well," the captain said, "but be back in an hour."

Mike headed down the path. . . .

"Soldier!"

"Yes, sir . . ."

"When you get back, you'd better get some sleep."

"Sleep—sleep . . . I can't sleep. . . . I can't sleep. . . . They won't let me sleep. . . ."

The Aussie captain stared after him, puzzled, as he swayed down the path to the village. Strange chap, this.

Mike stepped into a dirt square surrounded by a few dozen white stucco huts. In a moment he was engulfed by a half hundred peasants, women and little children for the most part. They all began jabbering at once, offering handshakes and back slaps of welcome.

Some kissed him. Some of the women cried.

Why do they cry for me? Don't they know the

British are beaten? Don't they know their saviors can't help them? Why do they cry for me? What strange people are these?

He took a kidskin of water from one of the peasants and the dryness loosened under the cool sweet taste of artesian water. It trickled down his chin and over his jacket. He poured it over his head and laughed, half-hysterically, as it revived him.

A woman shoved a loaf of bread into his hands and another gave him a cheese. He tore at the bread and stuffed it into his mouth and drank some more of the sweet water.

Another kidskin of water was given him and he looped its rope over his shoulder and stuffed his pockets with bread and cheese and thanked them all and shook their hands and kissed them.

The plane struck so fast no one heard it coming. It streaked from the sky and roared over the square, its machine guns ablaze.

A little girl of about four lay dead in the square, clutching a rag doll. She had pretty black curls and she held her doll tightly against her.

"Lynn," Mike whispered his daughter's name. . . . "Lynn."

The villagers began to edge back into the square. He could not face them. He turned and ran past the white huts onto the path.

"You there! I've been looking for you."

Mike whirled around.

A Palestinian sergeant walked up the path to him. "The captain sent me for you. We're going to push on."

"The plane—killed a little girl. . . ."

"I said we're moving out."

"Moving out? But—but it's still daylight—the planes will find us. . . ."

"New orders by radio. Hop to it."

"The man," Mike whispered, "don't let the man get me. . . ."

"What man?"

"The little man—the little man with the horn-rimmed glasses . . ."

"There is no man," the sergeant said.

"Yes—I saw him. I saw him coming through the grove. . . ."

The sergeant frowned. "You feeling all right, cobber? Come on now, let me help you."

Mike fell against the sergeant. The Palestinian steadied him and helped him back to the lemon grove where the troops were griping and muttering as they struggled into their packs.

The sergeant looked at the Aussie captain and shrugged, and the captain nodded knowingly.

"Just our blooming luck."

"I'll keep an eye on him, sir," the sergeant said.

"I saw him coming through the grove. . . ." Mike mumbled.

"Steady, cobber. steady."

They moved on.

The Palestinian sergeant stayed close to Mike and never took an eye off him. As the terrain became steeper and more rugged, Mike was alternately encouraged and prodded to keep on. When his strength gave out completely he was dragged. The Aussie captain led his weary troops toward a craggy mountain pass toward the coast. The endless day slugged on into an endless night.

"They'll get you. . . . They'll get you. . . . They'll get you. . . ."

Dawn of the fourth day brought them staggering from the mountains to the coast. They made for a beach not far from the city of Nauplion. The trek was called to a blessed halt in a woods behind the beach. Another group of a hundred men was already there and rumors flew wild.

From their hiding place they could see the town beyond the stretch of beach—what was left of the town. Once it had been the capital of a republic. A picturesque ancient fortress jutted out into the Gulf of Argolis and once the fortress had been known as the Gibraltar of Argolis. But that was once upon a time in another age and another war. In this war the Gibraltar of Argolis was a useless pile of rock against the vultures in the sky. Nauplion was bombed to the ground.

The Stukas were at it again, playing havoc, their scream overhead continuously.

The group dispersed and sprawled on the ground in weariness. Mike Morrison had reached an exhaustion beyond exhaustion. The days without sleep hung over him like the blade of a guillotine. He crawled away from the soldiers until he found a clump of thick shrubbery and he buried himself under it. He lay there, unable to move. His eyelids fell like heavy weights. He was unable to fight any longer. A deep slumber overtook him.

A beam of sunlight struck Mike's eyes. He blinked them open and propped up on his elbows. He pushed aside a branch and saw the fading sun. He had slept most of the day.

He yawned and stretched. His whole body ached, but his mind was clear. His gradual recovery from the stupor made him aware of the physical pounding he had taken in the past few days. He eased off his shoes and discovered that his feet were a mass of blisters.

He removed the kidskin from his shoulder and took a long swallow, then splashed some water over his face. He ate some of the bread and cheese, then gently worked his shoes back onto his feet.

The woods was strangely silent. There was no one in sight. He got to his feet unsteadily.

A far-off sound of cheering and singing brought him to alert attention.

He worked his way through the trees toward the sound as it continued to grow louder and more boisterous. Mike halted at the edge of the woods. Stretched across the shallow beach he saw hundreds of men. Units had been coming through the mountains for this rendezvous all day, he thought.

The sun was sinking fast into the bay. . . .

A ship stood offshore, blinking out a message.

Mike caught snatches of the men's talk.

"Prince Line steamer . . . An eight-thousand tonner . . ."

"The *Slamat* . . ."

"We'll evacuate as soon as it turns dark."

"I knew the bloomin' navy would come through . . ."

Michael Morrison closed his eyes and sighed. "Thank God . . . Thank God . . ."

He retreated into the woods several yards, found a hiding place and waited. Best not to take a chance. There were a thousand men milling around. Mosley and the little man would certainly be there.

The sun made a final burst into the horizon.

Mike knew he had to be cautious, but he was filled with optimism now. He'd get aboard the ship, all right, one way or another. Mosley and the little man would be watching the boats load on the shore. He'd cross them up. He'd swim out part way to the ship and have one of the boats pick him up. Mike was a strong swimmer. . . . In the dark Mosley and the little man would never be able to spot him from the beach. Once aboard, he'd get to the ship's captain—it would be all over soon.

He began to think of the reunion with his children and he almost wept with excitement. Mike thought of other things too. A shave and a shampoo at Kastrup's Barber Shop. He thought about a double filet mignon at Amilio's and he thought of the Top of the Mark. Maybe he'd just sit up at the Top of the Mark for three or four hours and look down on the hills of San Francisco.

The clothes and other things at the Kifissia Hotel weren't too important—insurance would cover the loss. But the pipes . . . Mike hated to lose his pipes. Well, no matter. He'd find some good Barlings and Petersens in London.

It was completely dark now.

Mike crept toward the water but kept a full hundred yards distance from where the troops had fallen into formations. Soon the boats would be coming to get them.

He removed his clothes and emptied the last bits of tobacco from his pouch. The pouch was waterproof. He slipped off his shoes and then went through his pockets. The passport—money—the little white envelope. Mike stuffed them into the tobacco pouch and zipped it shut. He was ready for the swim to the boat.

An hour passed.

The wave of optimism on the beach ebbed into a feeling of uneasiness. An hour later conversation was down to a feeble hum which gradually dwindled to a few suspicious whispers. . . .

A signal light cut the darkness. . . .

A buzz of voices grew louder and louder and advanced up the beach like a flock of hornets.

"The ship's aground on a sand bar!"

After a while the buzzing voices stilled and the eyes of a thousand men were fixed on the water. The silence was broken only by a stray prayer. . . .

"Break loose, dammit! Break loose!" Mike pleaded.

Through the midnight hours the thread of hope grew thinner and thinner. It became obvious even to the most obstinate that she'd never pull away from the sand bar in time to load a thousand men.

Morrison retreated to the woods again. He flung the pouch to the ground. "Son of a bitch!" He slipped into the British uniform. . . .

No time to while away in self-pity now. There's more than enough of that out there to take care of me, he thought. Well, for damned sure the British Expeditionary Force was in trouble—real trouble and sinking deeper into it with every minute that passed.

A move had to be made. He couldn't go on evading Mosley or the little man indefinitely. Another day— another hour? They'd catch up with him sooner or later. And in his anger he thought of his children. He did not want Jay and Lynn orphaned and forever wondering about the mysterious and unexplained disappearance of their father.

It would be dawn soon. Mike thought feverishly. Perhaps they had given up looking for him in Athens. There was still time to reach Athens. The Greek Army and British rear guard were still holding north of the city. If he could break free from here, he could shake Mosley and the little man. He would make for Nauplion and he'd shed the uniform. From there it would take only two or three days to get to Athens. The people were friendly; they'd help him along the way.

A crack of light on the horizon heralded a new day.

"Come on, lads, back to the woods."

Soldiers slowly began filing back to the cover of the woods, too dejected to talk.

Mike skittered away from them, dodging continuously to keep out of sight. He stopped for a moment to watch the sun rise. The ship sat out in the water, just beyond reach, as helpless as a turtle on its back. The crew was rowing frantically ashore. The light of day was accompanied by the drone of motors in the sky.

Not many minutes later the *Slamat* was blown to hell by Stukas.

Morrison saw the Aussie Captain and the Palestinian Sergeant walking in his direction. He ducked behind a tree, but he heard their voices as they passed.

"Have you heard the latest report, Sergeant?"

"What report, sir?"

"The Germans have entered Athens."

TEN

The full weight of the news crashed down on Michael Morrison. He was filled with self-pity. It was not his war, he protested silently, why should he be trapped in this thing that was not his doing?

The Germans would regroup at Athens, and a day, maybe two, would find them rampaging down the Peloponnesus. The enemy in the sky would not be the only menace now.

A motor convoy of thirty trucks came to a halt on

the dirt road a quarter of a mile from the wooded area.
All organization seemed to disintegrate. The soldiers
poured from the woods and boarded the trucks. They
needed no prodding from the NCO's to hurry.

Mike had to make his choice quickly. It was simple
... stay or go. Stay? Then what? Walk into the face of
the German Army? He'd never get to Athens now. If
he did—what good would it do? They'd have an air-
tight watch on the Embassy. They would be in command of the rail depots—the highways ... They'd have
every American in Athens under scrutiny. . . .

Mike watched the soldiers scramble aboard the
trucks. They pulled out one by one. . . .

No choice but to join them. Take the ever-narrowing
gamble that Mosley and the little man would not find
him. Take the slim, slim chance the British might yet
escape.

He hustled through the woods to a point where the
road ran close. The trucks sped by. As the last truck
bore down he stepped into its path and waved. The
vehicle slowed enough for him to race around back. A
half dozen reaching hands pulled him in.

Mike looked around quickly. Mosley and the little
man were not aboard. In a moment a cloud of dust was
churned up. He'd be safe—for the moment.

Near the highway junction below Nauplion the convoy joined another larger convoy. Hundreds of trucks
jammed with men of the escaping B.E.F. These were
men from the British, Australian and New Zealand
divisions which had been in action north of Athens at
the pass of Thermopylae. Outflanked, when the Greeks
failed to move the majority of their army back from
Albania, the British were forced to retreat below
Athens. They had fought stubbornly and bravely
against crushing odds from the sky and on the ground.

There were rumors that they withdrew mainly to save Greece from further ravage.

The divisions raced back into lower Greece, leaving an expendable rear guard at Corinth in hopes it could seal off German entry into the Peloponnesus while the bulk of the forces escaped.

Out of dozens of small ports and inlets in Southern Greece ships of the Royal Navy and of the British and Greek Merchant Marine worked a desperate evacuation of the fifty thousand trapped British troops. Harassed from the air and now pressed on land by the Germans, they worked to salvage their men from the doomed country. They evacuated by night, but many of the ships met the fate of the *Slamat*. Other ships escaped with their precious cargoes to Crete and to Lybia in North Africa.

A thousand rumors flew the length of the convoy. The King of Greece had escaped by flying boat. . . . The Greek Prime Minister had committed suicide. . . . The British had won a naval victory over the Italians. . . . The bulk of the Greek Army was captured in Albania. . . .

Then, heartening news. Most of the B.E.F. was being successfully evacuated. There was hope!

The long convoy grew at each junction. Eventually it switched from the vulnerable main highway onto a treacherous mountain road.

The trucks rattled, twisted and snake-turned along the nearly impassable route. They alternately hovered over deep gullies, grunted up twelve-degree grades and groaned down them in low gear. The convoy was completely shrouded in choking clouds of dust. The heat of the midday sun beat through the dust.

In the swirl of events that were to become part of history's darkest hours, a lone man, Michael Morrison,

American novelist of sorts, found himself rattling in a truckload of human misery. Without identity—running . . .

Why was he running? He did not know. There was a reason for everything, he had told himself often. There had been a reason for his wife's death. Through her passing he had reached maturity and stature as a writer. What was the unknown force that had hurled him into this flaming background? Perhaps some day he'd know.

But why me? he thought. It is not my war.

But was it his war any less than the soldier's hanging onto the tail gate for dear life? The soldier who was once a sheep rancher in New Zealand? Surely the New Zealander wonders why he is in Southern Greece. . . .

Or was it his war any less than the young Britisher's who hung over the side and vomited—or the big Arab's who stood next to him?

Or was it his war any less than the little girl's who lay in the village square clutching her rag doll?

He continued to wonder and stopped feeling sorry for himself.

Darkness enveloped the mountains.

The troops had been tossed around in the trucks to a point where they could no longer feel pain or exhaustion.

The single file of trucks crept through the towering mountains toward the sea. An endless stream of headlights winding, rising, falling. A stream that looked like pilgrims, carrying lighted candles, wending their way to the Holy Land.

Blood-curdling screams pierced the night when a truck would miss a hairpin turn and plunge its human cargo over a sheer cliff.

Many vehicles balked and broke down. The men had

to roll them over the side and the trucks would clatter
down a gorge and burst into flame. Cramming aboard
already crammed trucks, men hung from wherever they
could get a toehold.

The macabre procession rolled on. . . .

Daybreak!

A hundred trucks smoldered in the ravines below the
convoy.

The Dunkirk on Wheels came down from the mountains and stopped near the town of Kalámai on the
Gulf of Messína. This was the end of the line. There
was no place farther to run.

Michael Morrison saw the faces again—the faces of
the Greek people. And he wondered. Kalámai, an
open city, defenseless, was an ash heap.

The troops scattered through the many lemon
groves near Kalámai. Overhead, hundreds of planes
began to bomb and strafe every square foot of the
already gutted area.

Mike flung himself to the ground. Hour upon hour
the Stukas screamed and roared without letup. As the
world flamed around him a sudden and deep hatred
surged through him. He now knew his enemy.

Midday. The air raid continued.

A corporal wearing a British shoulder patch crawled
up to Mike and shook his shoulder.

"Come on, cobber," the corporal said. "We need
some men. There's a truckload of provisions stranded
in Kalámai."

Mike wriggled along behind the corporal. Over-
worked medics and doctors worked feverishly nearby
on the increasing number of casualties. The corporal
rounded up another ten men.

"Any news about the evacuation?"

"I heard they won't be able to get any ships around here till tomorrow night."

"What about the Hun?"

"Our rear guard is still holding at Corinth."

They worked up to the edge of the grove. A truck was waiting. The men broke for the truck, jumped aboard as it raced off toward Kalámai.

The truck rolled into the square. Three Stukas spotted it immediately. The working party quickly scattered over the cobblestones as the planes tore in. In a second the truck erupted into flames.

Mike dashed across the square. Suddenly his feet flew out from under him. He had stumbled over a dead horse. He lay there for several seconds, mesmerized, looking into the animal's eyes. They seemed to be mocking him, saying, "It isn't my war, either." Mike backed away from the horse and ran for a row of nearby houses. As a rack of bombs hit the square he half-threw himself down a flight of steps into a cellar.

Cowering against a wall were an old man and three women. One woman clutched a screaming infant. She tried to soothe the baby by putting her breast to its mouth, but each new bomb burst made the baby scream louder. The old man crossed himself and prayed softly. Another woman was becoming hysterical. Mike turned his eyes from the sight.

Three hours passed before the planes ceased the attack. Mike staggered from the cellar into twilight. The ashes of Kalámai smoldered. The dead horse with the mocking eyes was still lying in the town square.

Mike stumbled down the road from town. A passing truck stopped for him and drove him to a woods which ended about a mile from the sea. Here, the remains of the late British Expeditionary Force awaited evacuation.

Night brought a torrent of rain.

Michael Morrison was too tired to eat the last of his bread and cheese—or to think—or to care. He fell asleep in the mud.

ELEVEN

The morning sun poured its warmth on Mike. He rolled around in the slop, half of it caked solid on him. He dug the mud from his eyes and mouth and hair and sat up.

The troops were awake and slowly dispersing to nearby hills which would afford better protection.

Mike was prodded on by an NCO and followed the men up the slopes. On a low rise he borrowed a trench tool, scooped out a small foxhole and sat in it.

From his vantage point Mike could see an endless stretch of the bay. Directly below him nestled the town of Kalámai, close to the water, with neat lines of lemon and olive trees and vineyards, and beyond, the rocky backdrop of the mountains of the Peloponnesian range.

How peaceful it all looked from the hill! Even the planes that flew over Kalámai appeared like harmless little flies. His bread was soggy and inedible, but the cheese was still good. He ate it and drank the last of his water.

For some strange reason the vision of a dead horse and a little girl clutching her rag doll would not leave him. A chill passed through him, a strange sensation that he was on Twin Peaks looking down at San Francisco . . .

A nearby soldier generously offered Mike the butt of his cigarette. Mike thanked him and began to puff away.

"Hear the Germans have bridged the canal at Corinth."

That meant the XII Army was already in lower Greece. Unless the British rear guard could pull a miracle they would have to evacuate tonight.

Mike stretched out in his foxhole and looked at the blue sky above him and thought of the dead horse in Kalámai. He thought of the whole fantastic adventure. Almost unconsciously his hand reached inside the breast pocket of the khaki tunic. He held the small white envelope up to his eyes.

He frowned as he studied it. Scrawled in Fotis Stergiou's elegant hand, the envelope read: Sir Thomas Whitely—12 Beauchamp Place, London S.W. 3. *Kindly deliver in person.*

Mike fidgeted with the envelope for several moments. He bit his lip as the impulse overwhelmed him.

He ripped the seal open and his fingers dug inside nervously. There was one small folded sheet of paper. He sat up and unfolded the sheet.

In Stergiou's fine writing, there was a list of names and cities. The reverse side was blank.

He looked at the names listed. Obviously not Greeks —if they were, this was some type of code. Mike was a bit deflated. By this time he expected no less than some secret formula. . . .

He read down the list of names:

Jon Petersen, Johannesburg, S.A.
Lorrie Daniels, Sydney

> Elmer Jackson, Montreal
> Sarah Moonstone, Montreal
> Adam Piper, Montreal
> David Main, Christchurch, N.Z.

And on down the list—names—cities.

Mike was burning with curiosity. Who were these people and what was the meaning of the list? Each new guess only made him the more curious. Well, one thing was certain. Whoever they were was of extreme importance to both the British and the Germans.

The people who were after these names certainly put no price on human life. If the names were found on him, he was as good as dead. What if the names were not on him? He might have a chance even if the evacuation didn't come off. Suppose he memorized the names—it would be simple—only take a few moments . . .

There was another reason in back of Morrison's mind. A reason he would not even admit to himself. The experiences of the past days had done much to knock the spirit of neutrality from his soul.

No, the hell with it, he thought. I'll hang onto the list as long as I can and destroy it if the going gets rough. By memorizing the names I'd be committing myself.

But—if the list is destroyed it means the British will never get it.

Mike stretched out again, but the names of the people on the list would not leave him in peace. They kept rolling over and over in his mind—Jon Petersen—Lorrie Daniels—Elmer Jackson . . .

He sighed and wondered if he was crazy. He memorized the list, tore the paper to shreds and scattered the pieces to the wind.

The day passed without incident and as it moved toward sundown Mike knew the Stukas would leave the area. He looked over the vast expanse of water and on the horizon saw the first of many little black dots.

Ships were moving into the Bay of Messína!

The soldiers clambered from their foxholes and stared. This time there was no singing or cheering—only prayer.

Their prayers went unanswered as a frantic message bolted up the hill from mouth to mouth.

"German paratroops have landed on the outskirts of Kalámai!"

The NCO's and the officers were up and shouting.

"Everyone with a rifle, up to the front! The rest of the troops get down on the beach!"

"Come on, lads, everyone with arms! Move up!"

"Let's give the bloody Hun a show!"

The hills were angry!

First, in twos and threes, then in dozens and hundreds they poured toward Kalámai with murder in their hearts. Maddened, infuriated men held their rifles at fixed bayonets. Pistols, Bren guns—some with clubs

• • •

Under a bitter, unyielding offensive the Germans were driven from Kalámai.

The enemy regrouped and drove back the outnumbered British and Anzac rear guard with overwhelming force. The rear guard fell back into the town slowly, bleeding the Germans for every inch of ground. Darkness fell on the raging battle.

Destroyers and transports steamed into the Gulf of Messíni and stood by, waiting to snatch their soldiers from the enemy.

Mike Morrison ran down the hillside, desperately

determined to get aboard a ship and get out of Greece. When he reached the beach all semblance of discipline had broken. The unarmed men were in a frenzy to escape. Mike stood on the fringe of a howling mob two hundred yards deep and every man had but one thought.

Mike had to reach the water. He had to be there when the boats came. Behind him he could hear the sounds of battle coming closer and closer. . . .

He hunched his shoulders and rammed into the mass of hysterical humanity. He plunged deeper and deeper into the chaos, calling on every ounce of strength he had. Flailing arms—pushing—shoving—howling men . . . He flung men to the right and to the left of him. A surge of pushing men forced him to his knees. He struggled to his feet and stepped over bodies being half-trampled to death. Mike began punching and kicking—fists—feet—elbows . . . Another tangle of arms and legs brought him crashing into the sand with the weight of twenty men atop him. He bit and clawed his way free and burst through the last yards, plunging into the water. . . . He arose, knee-deep in water, gasping for air. His uniform was in shreds. His face was bleeding and his hands were swelling.

Suddenly it became very still.

A British colonel stepped out into the water in front of the men. His bearing was regal, but he could not hold back the tremor in his voice. "We are prisoners of war," he said softly.

The thread of hope had snapped!

> "Keep the home fires burning,
>   Though our hearts are yearning,
>   Though the boys are far away,
>   They dream of home . . ."

Half in shock, half to bolster their spirits, the men set up a dirge-like harmony which drifted up and down the beach.

Three words drummed over and over in the minds of thousands of stunned soldiers on the outskirts of Kalámai—prisoner of war—prisoner of war—prisoner of war . . .

> *"There's a silver lining,*
> *Through the dark clouds shining . . ."*

The glow of campfires studded the beach. Michael Morrison trembled as he sat by a campfire. He was frightened beyond any fear he had ever known. He visualized a black club smashing down on his head and men kicking at his ribs and throwing water on his unconscious body to revive him for further torture. He wanted to believe he had courage—but he was afraid.

He toyed with the idea of trying to bargain for his life in exchange for the names on the mysterious list. He tried to justify it in his mind, but he couldn't. He knew he would never know a minute's peace of mind for the rest of his life if he broke in cowardice before them. He chewed at his fingernails and tried to contain the queasy rise in his stomach. He dragged himself away from the campfire. He wanted to be alone with a few precious thoughts before the dawn came.

Through the long night, Mike sat withdrawn, reliving many wonderful hours in memory. He was with Ellie again on the Cal campus. . . . He was plunging into the Stanford line, fighting every inch of the way for the touchdown. . . . He held an infant in his arms. . . . He opened a letter which said, "We are happy to accept your novel. . . ." Yes, there were lots of good things to remember.

The first gray light of day was breaking through the darkness. A strange and wonderful calm took possession of him. He was no longer afraid. . . .

From the edge of the woods a tall blond man wearing a New Zealand uniform looked at Mike quietly.

The sun began to rise on the Gulf of Messína.

The tall blond man stepped from behind a clump of trees and walked up behind Mike's seated figure. Mike sensed his presence and turned to look up into the cold blue eyes of Jack Mosley. He was not startled—nor was he frightened. It was a calm acceptance.

"All right, Morrison, stand up—no outcry—move into the woods."

Mike arose and preceded Mosley into the woods until they were isolated from the beach. Mosley produced a pistol and leveled it on Mike as he leaned against a tree. His haggard face cracked into a smile.

"Touché," Mosley said with a mock salute of his pistol. "Your little drunk act was quite convincing, I must say. Threw us all off for a while." Mosley lit a cigarette. "Touché again on the merry chase."

Mike was silent. His eyes narrowed in hatred. He waited for Mosley to relax for only a second.

"You'll be interested to know that I got through the lines last night after the surrender. I had a phone chat with our mutual friend, Konrad Heilser, in Athens. He was quite overwhelmed with joy that you hadn't departed from this pleasant little country."

"If you're going to kill me, get it over with," Mike said quietly.

"Kill you? Oh, dear, no. Herr Heilser has such a lovely reception planned for you in Athens. I believe you have a bit of information he'd like. I do hope our car for Athens won't be late . . ." Mosley sighed. "Soon as the business of hauling your friends off to a prison camp is cleared we'll be underway."

"What are they going to do with me?"

"Do? Depends on you, old boy. You know, I have disagreed with Konrad about his messy methods of extracting information, but I will say this for him—he does get excellent results. By the bye, Morrison, would you give me the name of that splendid tobacco I smoked with you? I must send to America for some. . . ."

"You Nazi son of a bitch," Mike said.

"I say, you are a bad loser, Morrison," Mosley shrugged. "You know how it is in this business."

"You Nazi son of a bitch."

"Better save the endearments for Herr Heilser," Mosley said, smiling.

A sharp crack of a pistol report sounded.

An odd expression came over Mosley's face. His pistol spun around on his finger. His hand opened and the pistol dropped to the ground. Mosley wavered. He took a step toward Mike—another . . . His knees buckled and he fell to the ground and rolled over at Mike's feet. Mosley kicked and twitched. Then he lay still. His mouth fell open, the expression of amazement still in his dead eyes.

TWELVE

Every muscle in Morrison's body tightened.

He stood over the prostrate body of Jack Mosley and stared down on it, wild-eyed.

A man stepped from behind a tree a few feet away. He was a little man, only five feet tall and he wore horn-rimmed glasses and there was a smoking pistol in his hand.

The little man stooped quickly and went through Mosley's pockets. Then he rolled the body over to a small clump of underbrush. He picked up Mosley's pistol and shoved it into Mike's hand.

"Hide this under your belt," he said.

Mike continued to stare at the body.

The little man shook Mike, then took him by the arm. "Come on, mon," he said, "we've got to get out of here." Mike, still dazed, was half-dragged through the woods. They circled about and approached the troops on the beach. The men were stacking their rifles for confiscation.

Mike slumped down on the sand and shook his head.

"We are in luck," the little man said. "No one heard the shot."

Mike looked up to the little man standing over him. At this point he wouldn't have trusted his own mother. The little man slipped down beside him and talked in half-whispers. Mike clamped his mouth shut.

"My name is Soutar. Major Howe-Wilken, may his soul rest in peace, was my partner."

Mike tried to comprehend what Soutar was saying, but one strange thought kept running through his mind. He had been running away from this man, positive he was working with Jack Mosley. Perhaps he and Mosley had staged a fake death scene in the woods to deceive Mike. No, it couldn't be. Mike saw the blood gush from Mosley's mouth.

"Morrison, this is no time to play coy. We've got high plannin' to do."

Mike kept his silence.

"See that road there. In a few minutes German troops will be comin' down it. They have a prison camp already staked out at Corinth."

"All right, be quiet then. Hold your tongue. Konrad Heilser will find you in two days. See if you can stay quiet with him. Look, Morrison, the Germans have burned down over a hundred villages. They've been killin' off civilians like flies. It's going to be brutal when they find they've bagged a brigade of Palestine Jews."

The man who called himself Soutar lit a cigarette. "Don't be a fool. I'd've killed you along with Jack Mosley if I thought for a moment you weren't the right sort. I heard what you said to Mosley."

Maybe the pistol is full of blanks, Mike thought. It seemed futile to resist him. He knew his name, who he was. Anyhow, he was certainly done for one way or another if this Soutar was a German agent.

His heart pounded. He opened his lips, still uncertain. "All right," Mike said. "I'm Morrison and I'm an American citizen. I've had it—I want out of this mess. I was sucked into it and I want out."

"That," Soutar said with an impish smile, "poses a bit of a problem. You may as well face up—you're in this up to your neck."

"Why?" Mike demanded. "Why?"

"Like it or not. You know, Morrison, sometimes we have little to say with the turns of our lives."

Mike pawed at the sand, feeling more confidence in Soutar now. The little man was right—Mike knew it. There comes a time when a man is forced to say to himself, "This is the way things are—try to make the best of it." He had to accept the fact once that Ellie was dead—that he'd never see her again. There are certain things that can't be fought with mere will power.

"All right," Mike whispered, "I'm in."

As they sat and waited for the German round-up, little Soutar related his story in his thick Scottish burr.

When the German army invaded Greece and Yugoslavia, he and Major Howe-Wilken were sent to Athens to get the Stergiou list. From the moment they landed they knew that the enemy had got wind of their plans. This was later confirmed when Soutar discovered that Zervos, a government clerk, had suspected and sold the information to the Germans.

Soutar and Howe-Wilken avoided making contact with Stergiou. They arranged, instead, to have the list passed to Morrison. Then they made their move as a cover to exclude Morrison from any suspicion.

Howe-Wilken went to Stergiou's home and Soutar set out to find a plane from Athens. Soutar, knowing he was being followed, spent most of the day leading his shadows up and down Athens and finally shook them to make his rendezvous with Howe-Wilken. When Howe-Wilken did not show up Soutar went to Stergiou's home. It was too late to get a military escort as the British were already withdrawing.

Soutar arrived at Petraki, 17, only a few minutes after Mike had run out in a drunken stupor. Howe-Wilken lived long enough to relay the fact that Morrison still had the list and hoped he would go to the Tatoi airdome.

The rest was known to Mike. Soutar lost contact at the airdrome during the raid—traced Mike to the train —lost him and continued his search in the retreating B.E.F.

"Of course I was at disadvantage," Soutar said, "never having seen you or knowing exactly what you looked like. But then your good friend Mosley solved the problem for me."

"Exactly who is Mosley?"

"Well, he had a half dozen aliases. Actually, he was an Oxford-trained German agent. He worked hand in glove with Heilser."

"This Heilser—I take it he is top dog . . ."

"Ah, Konrad. I've met him twice before. Norway first—then France. Crack man. Brutal—persistent. He'll hunt us down if he has to look behind every tree and rock in Greece. It's going to be no picnic, Morrison."

"Go on . . ."

"Not much more to it," Soutar said. "When I saw Mosley on the train I knew he was searchin' you out. Instead of lookin' for you I watched Mosley in hopes he'd lead me to you. He did."

Mike grinned. "Can't help but laugh a little at the way I've been trying to get away from you. . . ."

"Very good for a newcomer, Morrison, very good. But you've got a lot of learnin' to do. The list—you have it . . . ?"

"I learn fast. I memorized it and tore it up." Mike paused. "The Stergiou list—what does it mean?"

"Well, you might as well know. Fotis Stergiou, may God rest his soul, was one of the best-known barristers in Greece. When the Italians invaded Greece last winter, Stergiou contacted many officials in the Greek Government and posed a proposition to them. They were to turn collaborators if occupation become imminent. Seventeen men agreed to this. They are now working for the Germans as far as the world at large is concerned. All of them are in important positions—there are two or three cabinet ministers among them. Actually, of course, they are working for us. Waiting for us to contact them."

Soutar ground out his cigarette and looked off to the horizon.

"No man on the Stergiou list knows who the next one is. Each man works separately."

"Why?"

"In case the Germans find one out, they won't be able to bag the entire lot. We will still have the rest of them working."

"And you say the Germans got wind through a Greek traitor?"

"Yes—Zervos is his name. And from what I understand, he's as slimy as Heilser."

Mike remained quiet for several moments. He had seen the onslaught—the power of German arms. It seemed such a futile gesture. "These men—these seventeen men—what can they hope to do against what we have just seen?"

"Do?" Soutar said. "You are naïve, Morrison. Many a war has been won or lost in our business. Among them, they'll have access to secret documents— they'll know every move the Germans plan in this theatre—they'll know every submarine operating from a Greek port—they'll know every troop and gun they have. Do? I'll tell you what they'll do. This war will take a turn, one day—mark my words. And when it does the Undergrounds in Greece and the occupied countries will handcuff twenty-five German divisions and keep them from fighting at the fronts."

Mike whistled. "I guess it is more important than a secret formula."

"What?"

"Nothing—just thinking out loud."

"When the day of reckoning comes these seventeen

men must be vindicated. They must not die as traitors. You are the only living soul who knows who they are."

Then Soutar grabbed Mike's hand. "Quiet," he ordered.

A lone German soldier edged cautiously down the road onto the beach and stood before thousands of his enemy. The British stared curiously at the foe they saw face to face for the first time.

"The names," Soutar whispered, "tell them to me."

Mike smiled. "Not on your sweet life."

"No time for that, dammit," Soutar said.

"I just figure you'll work a little harder at keeping me alive and getting out of Greece, Mr. Soutar."

"You do learn fast," Soutar sighed. "We'll argue about it later."

The German soldier barked an order in a half-frightened tone. The humiliated, embittered men of the late British Expeditionary Force fell into formations, grumbling.

Soutar's all-knowing attitude did much to calm Mike. The two, the tall husky American and the little Scotsman moved into one of the lines.

"What do we do?" Mike asked.

"With any luck at all we won't be shaken down again till we reach Corinth. Drop your passport and any identification first chance you get."

"What happens after we get to Corinth?"

"We're not going to Corinth, mon. We're going to jump the prison train."

Mike remembered the ground whistling by him on another recent train ride. He didn't like the idea.

The line began to move out toward Kalámai. German troops appeared, bayonets fixed, and fell in on both sides of the British.

"Stay close to me," Soutar whispered. "If we get

separated you are to contact Dr. Harry Thackery at the American Archaeology Society in Athens."

"Dr. Thackery—American Archaeology Society," Mike repeated.

Soutar shoved a hefty roll of drachmas into Mike's pocket.

The line reached the outskirts of Kalámai. The living dead of Kalámai stood in the streets and wept as the living dead of the B.E.F. marched sullenly through. The dead horse still lay in the square.

A halt was called at the half-wrecked train depot. German officers took over counting off the British in groups of eighty. The efficient enemy had already repaired the rail lines and a long line of cattle cars waited.

Soutar felt Mike's tenseness. He spoke to him softly and punched him in the ribs lightly and winked through his horn-rimmed glasses.

Crowds of Greeks gathered around the depot and wailed. The guards stretched out in an angry line to keep them separated from the prisoners.

A little girl pushed past the guards and walked toward Mike and Soutar's group. She held a loaf of bread in her hands. A guard curtly ordered her to stop. The British yelled for the child to go back. She kept coming—the bread outstretched for the hungry soldiers. Another order to halt ... She moved on. The guard lowered his rifle ...

Soutar grabbed Mike's arm to control him. "Turn your head—don't look."

Mike flinched as the shot echoed through the depot. British soldiers in screaming anger broke for the guard. Bayonets and clubs smashed them back into line. The loaf of bread rolled to a stop at Mike's feet. Soutar picked it up. "The least we can do—is eat it," he said.

The door to a cattle car was flung open.

"Quickly," Soutar whispered, "jump in the car first. Get up to the left front side. There's a small opening near the top." He nearly threw Mike into the car and scrambled in on his heels. In a second a flood of men poured in after them.

The door banged shut and they found themselves in semidarkness. They heard the ponderous bolt lock them in. They heard the guards climb to the top of the car to mount sentry posts.

Mike and Soutar were pinned in the corner by the crush of men around them. "Hold this position at all costs," Soutar whispered. The train jerked into motion, flinging them into a tangle of arms and legs.

Southern Greece is hot. Especially so from the inside of a cattle car. There was a stink of cattle, soon combined with a stink of sweat. An outbreak of vomiting started. It was impossible to move more than a hand or a foot. They were packed tight. . . . Everyone stood—to sit meant to be crushed to death. Sweat poured from them and they became parched from thirst and their bellies rumbled with hunger.

After an hour men began passing out. But they remained standing unconscious—there was no place to fall. Everyone began stripping, literally tearing his clothes off. Their bodies became slimy and rancid-smelling. The odors of urine and dung added to the agony.

In the next hour Mike buckled over a half dozen times. Soutar rubbed his temples and the back of his neck. When he blacked out Soutar slapped him back to consciousness. Now, nearly half the men were unconscious and the others groaned in agony.

The sweat fell into Mike's eyes, blinding him. Each

jerk of the train sent stabbing pains through him and a wall of men bashing against him.

In the late afternoon Soutar began to weaken. Mike had marveled at the stamina of the little Scotsman. He held Soutar up by the scruff of the neck. Soutar wheezed and gasped for air.

The blistering heat continued through early evening.

Soutar and Morrison alternated in keeping one another alive. There were two dead men in the car now.

Evening . . .

A fragment of blessed relief as it began to cool. The smell was long past the unbearable stage. Mike and Soutar had vomited till there was nothing left.

Men began to fall atop one another. The weak ones on the bottom, close to death, unable to move . . .

Darkness finally came. By now Mike would have jumped off a rocket to the moon.

"We go now," Soutar gasped.

"Suppose—suppose they stop the train?" Mike croaked.

"They won't risk it for one or two strays. If they stop they'll have a mass outbreak, and they know it. . . ."

Mike lifted Soutar to his shoulders. Soutar smashed the butt of his pistol into the screen. It ripped away.

"You go first—double back down the track for me. Allow a good two or three minutes for the train to pass."

Mike nodded.

"Give us a hand, lads, we're going to break for it."

Several pairs of hands were on Mike, lifting him. Mike caught hold of the top beam of the car. He swung his legs through the small opening. His hands slipped from the beam and the soldiers shoved him through.

The cool rush of night air was like a tonic. Mike's head cleared. He clung to the outside of the car, hoping the train would slow for a curve. But his grip gave way and he was hurled into space.

The ground came up and hit him with horrifying force. He bounced and rolled over a dozen times. Mike lay still for a few moments and then scampered down the rail bed and fell flat as the train sped past.

He looked down the line. He heard the crack of a rifle report. Mike didn't move until the sound of the wheels died and all he could hear was his thumping heart and muted breath.

Crouching, he scooted up to the tracks. How strange, how very strange, he thought. He felt no pain at all. Everything was wonderful and he felt lightheaded, as though he had drunk a half dozen martinis. He moved down the rail as if walking on a cloud. He felt good—real good . . .

He followed the ribbons of steel. It was dark, save when a quarter moon flirted in and out of a mass of clouds.

"Soutar," he called in a loud whisper, "Soutar!"

He heard a moan from the tall grass beyond the tracks. Mike crept toward the sound.

Soutar lay face down. Mike knelt beside him and turned him over. He was dead.

Mike went through his pockets. They were empty. He took Soutar's pistol and put it in his belt. He dragged the body over the tracks towards a woods. Soutar's legs dripped blood.

In the woods Mike dug a shallow grave, rolled the body into it and covered it with loose earth and branches.

Athens—Athens—get to Athens—Dr. Harry Thackery . . . Mike tried to stand but tottered against a tree. The woods started to spin as he wavered, trying to keep himself upright. I've got to get to the water—clear my head—stop the spinning . . .

He staggered through the woods to the beach. Down the beach he saw the lights of a village. People . . . Greek people—friendly—they'll hide me—get to the village . . .

The lights of the village began to spin madly.

Hurt—hurt in the jump . . .

On hands and knees he crawled closer to the lights, leaving a trail of blood in the sand. He touched his face —it was a gory mess.

At the first cottage, he struggled to his feet and fell against the door. He began to pound on it with inhuman force.

"Help me!" he screamed. "For God's sake, help me!"

The door opened.

Mike Morrison pitched in, unconscious.

Part 2

ONE

The phone rang. Konrad Heilser grunted, rolled over and fumbled for the lamp on the night stand. He pulled the receiver to his ear and dropped back on the pillow.

"This is Zervos," a voice said. "Forgive me for disturbing you, Herr Oberst, at this hour. I only this minute returned to Athens."

"Where are you?" Heilser mumbled, still half-asleep.

"Headquarters."

"Come up to my hotel at once!" He hung up rudely.

The naked woman next to Heilser cuddled up and groaned. He threw off the blanket and got out of bed. The girl's eyes opened.

"Where are you going, darling?"

"Business. Go to sleep."

She propped herself against the headboard and reached for the box of candy on the night stand. She pouted a bit to show her disappointment at his leaving. Deceitful little fool, Heilser thought, as he walked to the closet and took out a robe. The girl stretched her naked body sensuously to attract his attention but forgot to stop chewing the chocolate.

Lovely to look at, the little bitch, but she was becoming quite dull. Completely without imagination, she had no new tricks to hold him. He'd get rid of her next week and find another woman. One more on his intellectual level. One not so obviously greedy for the comforts he could offer. He walked toward the bathroom. The woman snuggled down beneath the sheet.

"Come kiss me, darling," she invited.

"Go to sleep."

The German splashed some water on his face and rubbed the sleep from his eyes. He applied some lotion to his hair and stared into the mirror for a long time. The usual look of self-admiration was gone. Zervos, the Greek pig, would be coming up with more bad news. Of that, Heilser was certain.

Zervos had botched the job miserably. First, he had allowed the old attorney, Stergiou, to commit suicide and so take the secret of the list to his grave. Second, Soutar had escaped. Third, the American, Morrison, had upset everything.

That damned American! There was nothing worse to contend with in this business than a desperate amateur. All the pieces fit toegther now. The American was used by Howe-Wilken and Soutar as a last-ditch measure. Already Heilser's office had been bombarded by a dozen inquires on Morrison's whereabouts.

Heilser had told the American Embassy quite truthfully that he wished he knew where Morrison was and that he was looking for Morrison day and night. He did not, however, mention what would happen when he found Morrison. The Embassy even went so far as to oblige Heilser with two pictures of the American. One from a dust jacket of a book, another from a passport.

Unfortunately one could not identify his own mother from such photos.

The trained agent takes certain paths, certain risks. The trained agent puts his mission above his life. Not so the desperate amateur. He will be unorthodox, develop the cunning of a wild animal to keep alive.

Heilser reconstructed the chain of events. First Mosley's call from Kalámai informing him that Morrison had not escaped from Greece and had been located in the B.E.F. After the call Heilser and Zervos had dashed to Corinth to await Morrison. Morrison had never showed up. Then, Mosley's body was discovered near the beach at Kalámai and Heilser knew the desperate amateur had won a round.

Next, Soutar's body was found near the railbed outside Nauplion. Heilser had questioned every prisoner and guard who rode the train. Working sixty hours without sleep, Heilser was able to establish the fact that Morrison had been on the train with Soutar and that they had tried to escape a few moments apart. Soutar had failed, Morrison had succeeded.

Here the trail ended.

A strange, unaccountable disappearance. Zervos had been sent to Nauplion with a team of men to question everyone there and in the nearby villages.

Heilser threw down the hair brush in disgust. He knew the price of failure to turn up the Stergiou list. He knew the work involved in trying to locate a desperate amateur.

Zervos stood in the drawing room with his hat in his hand. His envious eyes moved around the luxurious suite and stopped at the liquor cabinet.

He poked his head toward the half-opened door

leading to the bedroom. He could see the white sheets rustle.

Soon my time will come, Zervos thought. Reward from these German louts is small but a man can make his own rewards. He, Zervos, had played the right side. He had seized a grand opportunity. German occupation was a fact. A man does not want to be a government clerk all his life. To sell information was the right thing to do. Soon he would have a suite like this. The art collection he had taken from Stergiou's home was but the beginning of a fortune. Other things would come his way, now that he was a respected citizen.

He thought of some of the wealthy Greek citizens. He, Zervos, had the power of the German police behind him. Soon he would be paying friendly visits to these wealthy compatriots of his. He would advise them, in a nice way of course, that they were suspect by the Gestapo. But he, Zervos, could be their friend and benefactor and could arrange protection for them. Unfortunately, such protection would cost quite a sum of money.

It would not be long now—a suite—a girl in the bedroom to please him ... Perhaps he'd become the owner of an entire hotel. He would be rich and powerful. Not bad—not bad at all for a government clerk.

Zervos' dream vanished as Heilser entered and shut the bedroom door. For a second they exchanged stares of mutual hate, distrust and fear. The German opened the conversation with the customary sharp, "Well!" It never failed to make the fat Zervos flinch.

Zervos shrugged his shoulders and flopped his hands to his side in a helpless gesture. "He has disappeared into thin air. We have turned Nauplion inside out."

"Ridiculous!" Heilser said sharply. The German lit a cigarette and walked to the liquor cabinet. He offered

Zervos a drink only because he did not want to see him drool.

The fat man stood awkwardly examining the strange labels. One day he'd understand and enjoy these labels. He spotted a familiar-looking bottle of *retsina* and guzzled a half tumbler full then wiped his lips with his sleeve.

"I tell you, Herr Oberst, the man has vanished."

"Oh, shut up. There is nothing mysterious about it." Heilser set his Scotch and water on the table and started to pace. Then he sat at a desk and opened a large map of Southern Greece and drew a circle around Nauplion and its environs. "Someone inside this circle knows the answer." Heilser flipped the pencil on the table.

"But we have questioned a thousand people . . ."

"Then we question ten thousand more!" Heilser squashed his cigarette. "Do you know what kind of a man we are up against? We are up against a cornered rat. Nothing is more dangerous, more ingenious than a man who fights for his life." Then Heilser began to recite, as though he were speaking to himself: "One of two things will happen—we find him or he will come to us. He will try to get to Athens sooner or later. He will try to contact someone here. It will not be the Embassy. It will be someone Soutar told him to contact. Who will it be? Any one of a dozen known sympathizers of the British whom we already keep under scrutiny."

Heilser lit a cigarette and sipped his drink. "But we cannot wait for him to come to us. We go to him, slowly, quietly. We must not frighten him into the hills. He jumped a train moving at full speed. Unless he is a circus acrobat he is badly hurt and cannot move far or fast. I say he is still in or about Nauplion."

"If you say so, Herr Heilser."

"We agree on one thing, at least." He looked at Zervos and sighed in disgust. "It is obvious that I must go to Nauplion at once and conduct the search."

He arose and walked toward the bedroom. "We will find our Mr. Morrison, Zervos—we will find him if we have to look under every stone in your filthy country."

"Yes, sir."

Heilser opened the door and looked into the bedroom. "Wait in the lobby. I'll be down in an hour or so."

TWO

When he opened his eyes, everything around him was a dazzling white. The white-washed walls reflected a wash of golden sunlight. He shut his eyes, raised his hand to shade them, and opened them slowly again.

Staring down at him was a somber picture of Christ and a flickering candle burned beneath the picture. Transfixed, he looked at the picture several moments, then his eyes wandered to a half dozen ikons surrounding the picture.

He glanced around at the walls and stopped again and again to gaze at pictures of men with bushy beards or olive-skinned women with startlingly big black eyes. Scattered around the room were rudely built chairs and tables with a large loom in the center.

The brightness made a blur of everything and his eyes began to water. He felt numb. In an instant his mind flooded with recollections and he bolted up, then groaned, overcome by dizziness, and flopped back on the bed—a six-foot-wide bed built over an oven.

He heard a rustle at the other end of the room and sensed the presence of another person.

A handsome tanned girl of twenty stood over him. She had huge black eyes and a heavy bosom, and her jet-black hair fell softly onto a pair of smooth brown shoulders. He could see the separation of her breasts inside a low-cut blouse trimmed in fancy embroidery as she leaned over him. She wore a multi-colored skirt with a wide belt that reached clear up to her short bolero jacket.

"Help me up—I've got to get to Athens. . . ."

"Calispera," the girl whispered and ran from the room like a startled fawn.

Mike tried to struggle up but the slightest movement brought stabbing pains all over. Out of the corner of his eye, he spotted his clothes on a chair near the bed. He reached out and worked through the pockets until he felt a pistol which he placed beneath his pillow.

In a few moments the girl returned with two men. One was a giant and wore a heavy black cassock. It was almost impossible to make out his features through the brush of beard. He wore a long braid down his back and a high triangular black hat on his head.

The second man was short and stocky and bald except for a horseshoe fringe of hair. He sported an enormous, neatly waxed, handlebar mustache and wore a ballerina skirt with long white stockings banded in black around the knees. He had on a white blouse and a small cap falling away into a long tassel, and on his feet were pointed slippers with bright red pompons.

The ballerina man grinned at Mike and began jabbering in a strange Greek dialect. He wheeled about suddenly and issued a series of commands to an older woman who had just edged shyly into the doorway.

Another moment found the room filled with many men all looking at Mike with great curiosity. Then came several women carrying plates brimming with food—chicken, rice, olives, wine, a millstone-shaped loaf of bread.

The ballerina man drew a chair up next to the bed and poured himself a tall glass of wine and motioned Mike to eat.

Mike struggled to a sitting position, still speechless and staring about him, puzzled, a bit leery, mostly curious. The girl rushed to the bedside and adjusted the pillows behind his back.

Utter silence fell on the room as Mike examined the dishes before him. Everyone leaned forward. Mike's belly rumbled with hunger but he was unable to eat more than a few bites before he felt bloated. He shook his head and shoved the plates away. A wail arose throughout the room. The ballerina man argued passionately for him to eat but Mike tried to explain with gestures that he couldn't.

Then, the ballerina man abruptly ordered everyone but the girl from the room.

He turned to Mike and announced with much gusto in broken English, "I am Christos Yalouris, and this is my niece, from Dernica, by name—Eleftheria. My niece, Eleftheria, takes care of my aged mother in Dernica but I, Christos, personally sent for her to attend you. And what is your name?"

Mike's hand reached up and felt the bandages binding his head. His fingers traced a large scab which ran from his forehead to his jaw. "Athens ... I've got to get to Athens ..."

Christos shook his head slowly. "You have been very sick."

"I'm—I'm sorry. . . . Forgive me. My name is Jay—Jay Linden," Mike said. "Where—where am I?"

"You are in Paleachora."

"Paleachora?"

"Yes. Two hundred kilometers north of Athens."

"North? But—but—I was in Southern Greece. I don't understand?"

"You were found on the outskirts of Nauplion."

"But Nauplion is in Southern Greece."

Christos offered Mike some wine but he refused it.

"Many of you Englezos soldiers jumped off the prison train," Christos said. "The people knew it would be only a matter of a day before the Germans searched the place. Most of the other British soldiers moved into the hills."

"Go on, please."

"Fortunately, a member of my crew happened to be visiting the house in Nauplion when you came. You were unconscious and unable to move. You were put aboard my boat. I brought you here."

"Boat? You are a fisherman then."

"I, Christos, am sole owner of the mill in Paleachora," he announced with much pride. "I keep the boat for—er—trading—and other purposes." Christos winked slyly to indicate his boat was engaged in some sort of business not generally accepted as legitimate practice by the law.

Christos waved aside the thanks Mike tried to offer. "My duty," he said. "How do you feel? The doctor comes again in four or five days. You will rest."

"But—but I've got to get to Athens."

"We talk of that later. Come, Eleftheria, we let our friend Jay sleep."

The next few days were pleasant and restful. A steady flow of good food helped restore Mike's normal appetite. The assortment of aches and pains diminished a little.

Mike was grateful for the luck that brought him to Paleachora. Certainly Konrad Heilser wouldn't be looking for him in Northern Greece. At first he worried about being discovered but he learned that many British soldiers were hiding out in the hills. The Greek villagers greeted them with open arms. In fact, they deemed it an honor to harbor an escapee. Two Britons were already being concealed in Paleachora and others who had escaped en route to the Salonika Stalag passed through daily.

The Stergiou list tormented Mike constantly as did the recollections of the past weeks. The name of Dr. Harry Thackery did not leave his mind for a moment. But it was impossible to plan a move until he was on his feet. He examined his assets. Two pistols, a roll of drachmas and a valuable friend in the impish Christos. His passing as Jay Linden, soldier from New Zealand, went unquestioned.

The girl, Eleftheria, was close at hand during the day, weaving or spinning or working in the adjoining kitchen. She was terribly shy, too shy, in fact, to indulge in conversation. But a lifted eyebrow by Mike would send her flying to comply with his merest whim. She was so submissive that he fully expected her to throw herself across the bed and cry, "Beat me, master!" Eleftheria was pleasing to watch as she sat by the loom or flitted about on chores. Mike was too ill and too indebted to Christos and far too worried about the Stergiou list to entertain any ideas about the girl. None the less, Eleftheria possessed the natural qualities that could become disturbing to a man.

During the daylight hours, Mike saw little of anyone save for Eleftheria and Christos' lusterless old wife, Melpo. He didn't know if Melpo could even speak.

The village priest, Father Paul, stopped by now and again for a minute's conversation and every so often some male villager would poke his head into the room unceremoniously for a quick, "How are you feeling?"

Most of the women were of Eleftheria's variety. Well put together and, for the most part, lovely, but all were terribly shy. Once in awhile Mike would see a girl peek through his window but any attempt at conversation would send them scurrying down the road, giggling.

Mike looked forward to the evenings. Christos would return from the mill or from his numerous activities. A table would be placed near Mike's bed and they would share a candlelight dinner and talk for hours on end— about Christos. Other men would drift in and linger over a bottle of *krasi*. Christos' speech was always impassioned and punctuated by the slapping of his bald dome, hand wringing and arm waving while the tips of his curled waxed mustache quivered in staccato motion. Christos was the benefactor of all mankind. The local ward heeler, village big shot and general operator of all things. Being "Englezos," and having great understanding, Mike was brought in on many of Christos' little schemes and deals. The host always had a dozen things working for him. Now, with a war on, his boat would be able to haul more and more pay loads and already Christos was planning how he was going to corner property in Athens in exchange for wheat, which was certain to become scarce.

As evening turned to night and the wine loosened tongues the conversation always swung around to Christos' escapades in the whorehouses of the big cities. Then, after Christos would finish his story, each man in turn would tell of his experiences in the brothels. Mike learned that the prostitute held a position of respect in Greek culture. A wife, once wooed and wed, through family arrangement, was usually retired to the background. Her sole purpose in life was dedication to home and family. It was an accepted fact that a man could patronize the brothels whenever it suited him. The clever prostitute often found herself a husband who could provide comfort and respectability.

And when the hour grew late and the candle burned low Christos would offer his opinions on what he considered a real war. Dressed in his *funstanella,* he would pace the room and scoff at the German invaders as Johnny-come-latelies. The Bulgars, the Turks and the Italian Macaronades—these were the *real* enemies—as proven by centuries of warfare.

And Christos' epic would become a bit more exaggerated with each telling. . . .

All the men in his old platoon were dead, except for Christos and two comrades. An enemy horde had charged a hill which he was determined to hold. He and his comrades had hacked their way through a wall of charging Bulgarian flesh until he, Christos, stood alone—with two hundred of the enemy piled at his feet. At the close of the tale Christos' bald pate would be bright purple intersected by protruding veins. He would be panting and sweating as he lifted a broomhandle and ran it through the guts of the last Bulgarian.

"This is the way to fight a war! Man to man!"

In Nauplion, Konrad Heilser stood on the balcony of his hotel suite overlooking the Bay of Argolis. His eyes were bloodshot and his usually slick hair was a mess. The ash trays in the suite brimmed with half-smoked cigarettes. His necktie was loosened and his shirtsleeves were rolled up.

He had made a thorough search of Nauplion and was unable to uncover a single clue in the strange disappearance of Michael Morrison. Out of sheer desperation, Zervos had been sent on a mission, based on hearsay that a fisherman had overheard a conversation about a body being placed aboard a boat a day after Morrison had jumped the prison train. The fisherman was now somewhere among the myriad islands in the Aegean.

It was a straw, but Heilser was desperate. Zervos was sent to find the fisherman.

The phone rang. Heilser entered the living room and snatched it from the hook.

"A call for you, Herr Heilser."

"Hello, Herr Heilser?"

"Yes, speaking."

"This is Zervos."

"Where are you?"

"On the Isle of Kea."

"Did you locate the man?"

"Yes, I have him in custody. He is reluctant to talk, though."

"Does he know the American's whereabouts?"

"He knows something—that is certain."

"Bring him to Athens immediately. I go immediately. He will talk when I am through with him."

"Very well. I have a boat standing by. We will be in Athens tomorrow night."

THREE

At the end of a week, a doctor came from Dadi, unwrapped the bandages, examined Mike's injuries and declared him a very lucky young man.

Mike was anxious to test his legs for a day or two, then press Christos for transportation to Athens. With Eleftheria's help he wobbled from the cottage dressed in a coarse set of peasant's clothes. Melpo supplied him with a heavy cane. With the help of the cane and one arm around Eleftheria, he made his way from the cottage into the sunlight, through Melpo's vegetable garden and out the gate. Mike was terribly aware of Eleftheria's closeness, and forced himself to suppress some disturbing thoughts.

Out on the main square, he was mobbed with well-wishers. First the children came and ran off to get their parents. Mothers and daughters arrived from their cottages, and men dropped their plows and came from the fields. The square teemed with excitement.

And Michael Morrison, the cynic, the scoffer at sentiment, was deeply moved by it all. He tightened his grip on Eleftheria's shoulder and smiled and she made no attempt to hide her pride as a nurse.

Another two days passed and Mike felt his strengh returning. He increased the distance of his walks with Eleftheria, who was beginning to lose some of her shyness.

The village of Paleachora lay peacefully on the slope

of a hill within sight of the island-dotted Aegean Sea. It was very much like any other village in the province. A narrow crooked dirt road or two which wove in and among white-washed, thatched-roofed little cottages.

The Church of the Prophet Elias stood apart on a small knoll on which herds of goats and sheep grazed quietly under the watchful eyes of barefooted young shepherdesses.

Pine forests covered the hills, and the landscape was a peaceful tracery of vineyards, wheat fields and olive groves.

The quiet was occasionally broken by the thump of a crude wooden plow on the earth or the outcry of an infant lying in the shade of a tree while his mother worked in a nearby field or the grinding of the mill wheel or a bleating from the flock.

The village of Paleachora was at the northern end of the province of Larissa on the endless eastern coast of Greece.

Mike and Eleftheria would walk hand in hand past the Church of the Prophet Elias to a stream which flowed past a clearing thick with pine needles. In the peace and serenity of the pastoral scene he often found it difficult to concentrate on his Greek lessons. She would throw her head back and laugh at his efforts to pronounce the S and the Z with proper softness. But Eleftheria never laughed unless they were alone and out of sight of the curious eyes of the villagers. Mike would suddenly find himself patting her olive cheek, or, when he put his arm about her waist, he noticed that her childlike face acquired a sleepy feminine look. They would be silent for long periods. Then Mike would damn himself for being lulled by the loveliness of this girl and for letting his mind stray from his mission. After a third visit to the forest he knew he would have to make a decision.

He had little occasion to say more than "hello" to the two British escapees in Paleachora. Mike studiously avoided the transients who hid out in the church. He did get trapped into several conversations with an Australian who called himself Bluey. Bluey stayed with a family just a few cottages away from Christos'. His one claim to fame was a constant gas pressure on his stomach. Most of his sentences were punctuated by belching. Bluey, aside from repeating the story of his escape from the Stalag at Corinth, did reveal something of interest to Mike. It seemed that many wealthy Greek families in Athens had provided boats for British soldiers to escape to North Africa. Mike filed it as an ace in the hole should anything go wrong in his attempt to contact Dr. Harry Thackery.

For the most part, however, Bluey spent his time denouncing the English. . . .

"Leaves us stranded in this ruddy place, they did. Where in 'ell is the bloody Royal Navy, I asks you, Jay? Nothin' but one bloody Dunkirk after another . . .

"Not that I gots anything against the Greek people, Jay. They're as fine a lot of blokes as you'd come across anywhere, and the sheilas . . . But I tells you if it wasn't for us diggers, the Anzacs and the rest of the bloomin' Commonwealth troops the bloody Hun would be in London, that's wot—and they strands us 'ere. Who's goin' to do their bloody fightin' for 'em, I asks you?"

As a "New Zealander" and brother "Anzac," Mike was compelled to agree.

"You missed the 'ell 'ole at Corinth, Jay. . . . You're the lucky one. Every day we was buryin' the dead in lime pits. Scurvy-ridden place it was; every joker there had the bloody cruds. Jerry is a mean lot, that he is.

And I tells you wot happens—when I goes to make my first escape—who rats on me?—a bloody English doctor, that's who. . . . Even in an 'ell 'ole like Corinth they's got to have their snootin' ways. . . ."

Nothing as low as an Englishman, Mike agreed.

"I'm gettin' to Athens, that's wot, and find me a family to buy passage to North Africa."

When Mike inquired as to how Bluey would get to Athens, Bluey didn't quite know. Every train was loaded with inspectors. Travel passes were needed to budge an inch in the country and it was open season on escapees.

"Know somethin', Jay? You talks like those Yanks I seen in the flicks."

That, Mike explained, was because he worked for a shipping company in San Francisco for fourteen years. Nice place, America.

Ten days had gone by since Mike's arrival in Paleachora. After his own survey of the situation, he knew he was trapped unless Christos would help him get to Athens. He waited patiently for word from Christos that he would be taking his boat out again but no mention of it came. On the eleventh night Mike decided to take the initiative.

After dinner, Christos shooed Melpo and Eleftheria from the room and the two settled back with several bottles of *krasi* and some foul-smelling tobacco.

"Christos, my dear friend, when do you plan to leave again with your boat?"

"As soon as I find the right cargo. Many things move well these days. I wait."

"Christos. I'll put it straight. I've got to get to Athens."

"You do not like it here?"

"I like it here very much."

"Then why you want to leave? You damned fool. You'll get picked up for sure."

"You know why, Christos. I endanger the whole village. They burned a village yesterday for harboring an escapee. Besides, as a soldier, it is my duty to escape."

"The crop looks fine this year, Jay. I have a very profitable proposition being worked out. I will be able to get some property in Athens."

Mike gritted his teeth. He drank a swig of *krasi* and puffed on his pipe. "Well, anyhow, now that I'm all well again you'd better send Eleftheria back to Dernica. I know your aged mother must need her."

"My aged mother stays at the home of a brother. She is fine."

"But, what I mean, Christos, I no longer have need for a nurse."

Christos scratched his bald pate, poured more wine and stared at Mike as though he were a crazy man.

"You do not like the girl? She has done something wrong?"

"I like her very much."

"Then why send her back to Dernica?"

"Well—the fact is, I like her—well, maybe too much. It is a rather delicate situation. Well, look at it this way. You're a man. You know how things might happen. You see, I like you very much, Christos, and I wouldn't want to bring anyone any unhappiness."

"Jay, you talk like one damned fool."

"Well, what I'm actually trying to say—it might lead to complications if she stays."

"Complications! You say you like her?"

"Yes—but . . ."

"She wants to stay. You like her—settled, she stays!" Then, as an afterthought, Christos added, "Besides, my poor wife, Melpo, has been working too hard." This was the first time he had so much as acknowledged Melpo existed.

The two men stared at each other for several moments like stubborn roosters. Mike was disturbed by Christos' sly fox act.

"Why don't you go out and watch the dancers, Jay? Eleftheria wants to teach you the *syrtos* so you can dance too. . . . You like to dance?"

Mike shoved the chair back and stomped from the room. Christos looked after him with a childlike smile.

In the middle of the night Mike awoke in a cold sweat, his heart racing. He flung off the covers and walked to the window. He calmed down after awhile as he shook off the nightmare. For many moments he stared down the street of the sleeping village. In the next room he could hear Christos and Melpo snoring in rhythm. From the window he could see the barn where Eleftheria slept. He visualized her there on a cot and his mind traced every line of her soft body.

He spun away from the window in anger. He had allowed himself to be lulled into a fool's paradise. He was angry because he knew, deep inside him, that he did not want to leave Paleachora. Yes, Paleachora had become like an irresistible lure.

But in his nightmare the names of seventeen men had rumbled through his mind in the form of a roaring train and the click clack of the wheels said—Dr. Harry Thackery—Dr. Harry Thackery—Dr. Harry Thackery. Suddenly the train was in San Francisco Bay enshrouded in fog and he heard the voices of his children, Jay and Lynn, call in desperation from the water, "Daddy—Daddy—Daddy . . ."

Mike Morrison was trapped in heaven and he was angry. Christos hadn't fully played out his hand, but Mike surmised what was coming. Without the help of Christos, Mike was powerless unless he was willing to risk a walk of two hundred kilometers to Athens. Strange land, no travel pass, no personal papers, no friends. The odds would be crushing. Too crushing a risk for the Stergiou list. On the other hand, he could not press Christos into unfriendliness.

There was still another part of Mike's dream. A far-off chorus whispering, "They'll find you—they'll find you—they'll find you ..." Mike was frightened. He knew full well that each day in Paleachora brought Heilser closer. The German was not sleeping either and sooner or later a trail would bring him to the village.

Mike thought it through carefully and decided to give Christos another few days to calm down from this evening's fencing. Then he'd have to press Christos, even at the risk of daring the journey to Athens by foot.

He looked from the window once more to the stable where Eleftheria slept. Then he climbed into the huge bed over the oven and pulled up the covers. He lay on his back and stared at the blackness and heard the sounds of Melpo and Christos snoring. He could not sleep.

Konrad Heilser sipped his Scotch and water and lit another cigarette. The fat Greek, Zervos, sat next to him, rumpled and drowsy. Heilser looked across the broad polished table at the defiant fisherman named Maxos.

Maxos glared back at Heilser. His bulging muscles rippled through a tight-knit navy-blue sweater. His massive arms were almost black from years of whipping winds and burning sun. His face was square and hard and his hair fell in black ringlets and from his right ear hung a small circular gold earring.

Maxos was angry because he had been snatched from his boat by Zervos on the Isle of Kea. He could not fish and he could not drink *krasi*. Maxos did not care whether Mr. Heilser found whom he was looking for or—or if he did not find whom he was looking for. For Maxos was half fish, and away from his boat he was a fish out of water.

"All right," Heilser said. "Tell me the story once more."

"I have already told it fifty times," Maxos grumbled.

"I want to hear it again," Heilser said.

Maxos sighed. "I can go to my boat then?"

"Perhaps."

Maxos grumbled again. "I was in a waterfront saloon in Nauplion drinking and minding my own business. I had just returned with a catch of fine fish. A man should mind his own business."

Heilser ignored the rebuff. He was more interested that Maxos was in the saloon the same night Morrison jumped the prison train near Nauplion.

"A man was at the next table to me, drinking. He was minding his own business, too."

"You say you do not know who this man was?"

"I had seen him before about four months ago in the same saloon. He was a crewman from a boat that came from Larissa Province. He was dressed like a Larissa farmer and spoke with that accent too."

"You did not meet this man personally?"

"I tell you I did not. I tell you so a hundred times I did not. How many times you want me to tell you I did not?"

"Continue with your story."

"As I said—his boat came once before. Four months ago."

"What do you know about this boat?"

"Only that it was trading grain and tobacco and many other things, probably stolen. I do not trade with such people."

"How do you know about this boat?"

"From people around the docks. There is always gossip on the docks. People do not know how to mind their own business."

"And this is the second trip this boat has made to Nauplion. Are you sure it is the same boat?"

"I'm sure. I never forget a face. Same crewman."

"And you're sure it comes from Larissa Province?"

"I know a central province farmer when I see one."

"You were drinking—and minding your own business—then what happened?"

"A second man comes into the saloon and tells the man who is drinking he must return to the boat. They argue. The man who is drinking does not want to return because he is going to a whorehouse. Then the second man tells him to talk quiet. They had taken a passenger aboard and had to leave Nauplion at once. That is all. They leave and I mind my own business. Next day I go out again with my boat until he," pointing to Zervos, "comes to me on Kea and begins asking me all sorts of questions."

Heilser pressed a button which brought two German soldiers into the room. He nodded to them, indicating that Maxos was to be taken away.

"I can go to my boat now?"

Heilser did not answer.

"Fix me a drink," Heilser ordered Zervos.

"What do you think?"

"It is our answer, if there is an answer. In Nauplion we caught ten British escapees while searching for Morrison. If Morrison was in Nauplion we would have caught him too. He must have gotten away by water. He is the only one we can't account for who escaped in that area. Could the fisherman be mistaken about Larissa?"

"One Greek knows another. He is not mistaken."

"Obviously Morrison is injured. Obviously, he will sit it out for awhile in the central part of the country. He has tried to contact no one in either Athens or Salonika."

"He could be in any one of the thirty villages," Zervos said. "Can we raid them all at the same time?"

"Are you insane? There are over a hundred escapees in that area now. No, we weed the villages out one by one. It will not take long. Bring me thirty Greeks tomorrow and have them here in the morning. Also get a dozen Italian tourists. I'll see to it now that all troops are kept out of that coastal area. We do not want to startle him into the hills."

Zervos placed the drink before his master. "Do you wish me to file a complaint with the American Embassy about the Archeological Society?"

"No. If this Dr. Thackery is aiding British escapees let him continue. We have the place under twenty-four-hour scrutiny. I have a hunch. I don't often play them. Thackery has entered the picture late—just as Morrison entered late. I'll wager you that he is Morrison's contact."

FOUR

Mike loved to walk through the sloping vineyards and pick the full juicy muscats from the vines. He loved to sit in the shade of a pine and watch the old men and the boys trundle down the road under a load of firewood as they had done for centuries eternal. It was good to smell the sharp tang from the huge sacks of goats'-milk cheese and to stand on a hilltop and watch the stalks of wheat bend their golden heads. It was a delight to see the buxom, barefooted girls marching straight and handsome from the well, balancing heavy urns on their bare shoulders.

Most of all he loved the evenings when the sun dropped behind the pine forest. The shepherdesses, their crooks of office in hand, would amble down from the pasture along the narrow path surrounded by their bleating flocks. The air would be cool in the evening and a song would start on someone's lips. The melody would carry over the hills to be picked up by another singer, then another until all of Paleachora would echo with a harmony of voices in an ancient song.

The village had become a haven for Miachel Morrison. Although he kept fighting the voice that urged him to stay a little longer, he yearned for the contentment he had never known before.

The men would head for the coffee house and talk of big things and little things while the women prepared the evening meal. Soon they would sit around their crude wooden tables, say their evening prayers and eat blessed bread and chicken and a dessert of grapes. . . .

When the women finished their chores a fire would be built in the square and there would be dancing by its light. First, the gentle *sirton*—as gentle as the people of Greece. Then, when the flames grew higher and the wine burned deep, the dancing turned to the violent gyrations of the *calamatiano*. It grew wilder and wilder and the man danced themselves into exhaustion, egged on by roaring, shouting onlookers. There would be a glint in the eyes of the old men as they thought of the days when they could leap and spin, and they would jump into the ring for a fling at their lost youth.

One night Mike felt particularly high and leaped into the ring with Eleftheria and danced her into a state of exhaustion, to the shouting approval of the villagers. He ended his dance with a leap and a firing of both pistols into the air—then collapsed into Eleftheria's arms.

It seemed to Mike that the very soul of Greece danced by firelight.

After the dance, the women would be dismissed and the men would gather in the coffee house or someone's cottage and talk the night away. And Christos would retell his adventures in the whorehouses and his valiant stand against the Bulgarians.

Each day Mike learned more about this strange and wonderful land. The land from which sprang the ideal that has become the eternal striving of man—the ideal of freedom. From earliest days Greece had been a tormented land—tormented by Nature—famine, flood, earthquake—and tormented by man—conquest, war, civil strife. Blood ran deep in her soil. But the Greek was a man of steel. This latest scourge—the German conquest—this, too, would pass as the others had passed.

It was as though Greece was being put to the test during the ages for conceiving the ideal of freedom. The brief eras of peace and plenty were but interludes in the everlasting trial by fire. But anyone who has seen a man dance the *calamatiano* would surely know, as did Mike Morrison, that Greece would be free again.

The presence of British escapees in Paleachora became an open secret. Food supplies were running low in the big cities and every train to Dadi, the nearest terminal, brought city people scouring the countryside in search of food. They carried possessions, many of great value, to trade for wheat and other staples.

Christos and the other farmers were quick to capitalize on this tragic situation. Wheat went at fabulous price. When inflation made money almost worthless, barter became the means of exchange. Christos, as owner of the mill, hit upon a windfall. In return for wheat and other food products, he acquired possession of a half dozen properties in Athens.

Mike argued bitterly against this, but Christos reckoned he was doing the city folk a favor by keeping them alive. He added that the city people had always considered the farmer a second-class citizen and had cheated him for years.

As the presence of escapees in Paleachora became known, "big-town girls" from Dadi drifted to the village in search of fun with the British, whom they admired enormously. The city girls were not a bit shy. They had cast aside the age-old traditions of female inferiority and took pleasure in flaunting their equality before the farmers. The shocked villagers warned the

British boys that they were all tramps with venereal diseases or German spies or both. Mike seemed to agree with the latter explanation and kept clear of all outsiders.

Within a few weeks after the British collapse in Greece, hundreds of escapees roved all over the country and were accepted by the people with open arms. Even in the cities the people were sharing the last loaf of bread with escapees.

This situation became a major headache for the Germans. Even in their position of helplessness, the British gave hope to the people by their mere presence. Vicious counter measures were taken. Spies were planted, bribes were offered, traps set, threats were made. The Germans began using British turncoats as bait. Then came the announcement that any village found harboring an escapee would be burned to the ground. Still the British escaped and still the people took them in.

It all added up to one thing for Mike. His fool's paradise was truly a fool's paradise. Sooner or later some child would talk to one of the Italian "tourists" or one of the big-city girls. He had to break Christos down and make his move immediately.

Although the feeling in Paleachora was overwhelmingly pro-British and, even more strongly, pro-American, the effects of the occupation hit them fast. Taxation, a portion of the crops, and now their very homes were in jeopardy. The weaker ones buckled under the pressure and thought it best to keep the escapees moving. For even with the new tax the price of wheat was bringing them rewards never known before.

The majority favored resistance and believed it a sacred duty to shelter escapees. Other men vowed to burn their wheat fields before giving the Germans a kernel of grain.

But Paleachora was getting tense. Mike no longer enjoyed the visits to the coffee house. The arguments raged far into the night. Then, one day, suspicion and whispers supplanted song and dance when a nearby village was burned to the ground. Several families were suspected of having turned collaborators.

"We have found him," said Zervos' voice over the telephone.

Konrad Heilser bolted upright in bed. "Where are you?"

"Dadi."

"Are you certain?"

"I am positive," Zervos answered.

"Have any of our people actually seen him?"

"No, but I have a peasant here who informs for us. He speaks of a British escapee who talks like an American. His description of Morrison is perfect. Even to the degree that Morrison arrived by boat and was injured in a jump from a prison train."

Heilser's heart raced as he threw off the covers and told his new woman to go back to sleep. He began unbuttoning his pajamas as he spoke into the phone. "Where is he?"

"A village named Paleachora—northern end of the province. I wanted to check with you before taking a squad of soldiers to pick him up."

"No, wait a minute. A squad of men may be too small."

"I don't understand," Zervos said.

"I have a half dozen reports of villagers making armed resistance. We better not go in undermanned."

"What shall I do then?"

"How many troops will we need to cut off the village?"

"Two or three hundred," Zervos answered.

"Do nothing. I leave for Dadi this minute. We will organize a raid to hit this village in the middle of the night tomorrow."

Christos' bald head and waxed mustache shone in the candlelight. He held his hands to his heart.

"Jay, as I love you like a son, you should not leave."

"Be sensible, Christos. Another day—another two days—the Germans will burn Paleachora to the ground."

Christos spat on the floor and issued an oath against the Germans, then crossed himself. "Even if you are gone we will never turn our backs on the Englezos. . . . No! I will not let you leave!"

Despite Christos' shady dealings, he was a Greek to the core.

"I have this money—five million drachmas—take it," Mike said.

"You have insulted me. Do you think that all Christos cares for is money? You, Jay, are my friend."

"All right, then, I go alone."

Christos grumbled under his breath. "Five million drachmas—fifty million drachmas. You would think all Christos wants is money. If I had all the money I could carry in my boat, I could not buy a bag of wheat with it. I would give you my boat but it isn't fit to cross the sea. Besides, within one hour a patrol ship would find you. . . . Besides, I do not know the lanes over the mine fields. . . . Besides . . ."

"I'm not asking you to take me to North Africa. I only want to get to Athens—immediately."

Christos fiddled with his glass of *krasi* for a moment then lit his huge bowler pipe. He stared at Mike calmly and spoke without the usual breast thumpings.

"My niece, Eleftheria, is a nice healthy girl, no?"

Mike grinned to himself. Now, at last, Christos would play out his hand. He agreed that Elftheria was as healthy as a horse.

"You know, Jay, it is a custom in our country for a suitor to come to the father with a ring and the two to enter into a contract. I speak to you as her guardian. I have a plot of land in Dernica, very, very fine land, where my aged mother lives. I have a sizeable dowry for Eleftheria. You do speak Greek very well for the short time you have been here. If you were to return as her husband . . ."

Mike shook his head. "I am married and I have two children."

Christos arose and clasped his hands behind him. He looked like a little puppet pacing back and forth in his *fustanella*. He stopped and sighed.

"Jay, my good friend, I tell you something. From the minute I take you on my boat in Nauplion, I say to myself, here is a man. Here is a man who is something. I am now rich, although you may not agree with things I do. But every man wants this. He wants this for his son. Melpo has not given me a son. Jay, I would like very much . . ."

Mike arose and walked from the cottage through Melpo's garden and onto the dirt street. He could see Christos standing in the doorway in his ballerina dress looking after him. Paleachora was asleep now—a restless and troubled sleep, disturbed by the problems of war.

Mike walked to the hill past the Church of the

Prophet Elias and sat beneath a cypress tree and looked at the land by moonlight.

Many men follow a rainbow. But Mike Morrison had met it head on. Here was the sanctuary from reality that men dreamed of.

But he was filled with love as he thought of the hills of San Francisco. And he thought of the fog as it rolled in lazily or tore in angrily through the Golden Gate. He loved the redwood trees of Muir Woods stretching toward the heavens and he loved to watch the surf smash against the rocks below Land's End. But this love had always been a brooding, morbid love which seemed to turn to bitterness in the pages he wrote.

Greece had unlocked an inner door to a love of people that he had never been able to feel before.

For many reasons Mike wanted to return to Christos and say, "Yes, I'll stay. I will go to Dernica with Eleftheria and till the land and dance the *syrtos* and drink *ouzo* in the coffee house and I'll learn to sing as I come from the fields."

He began to laugh at himself, rather ashamed that he had been taken in by such a bad plot.

Christos sat at the table as he entered the cottage. Mike sat beside him and poured a glass of wine. They heard Melpo snore from the next room.

"I don't love her," Mike said.

"Bah! What are you talking about? For why you need love? She will have your children, she will make cloth for you, she will scrub your feet. Why you need love? You Englezos are all crazy! Do you want your women to be like—like those tramps from Dadi?"

Mike shook his head. Christos knew further argument was useless. With a look of hurt and sadness, he slammed his glass down. He sighed and started from the room. "Very well, very well. We sail for Athens at sunrise tomorrow."

FIVE

"Jay! Wake up!"

Mike rolled over and propped himself on an elbow. Christos, in long nightshirt and cap, with a candle in hand, stood over the bed. The candle quivered in his hand and his face was as waxen in color as his mustache.

"Eh—what's up?" Mike mumbled, half-asleep.

"A signal from the next village. German soldiers all over the area. They're heading for Paleachora."

Mike threw off the covers.

"Go to the church quickly!" Christos said.

Mike struggled into his clothes, checked his pistols and bolted through the door and crept close in the shadows of the cottages until he worked his way toward the knoll. He sprinted up the dirt path and through the door of the Church of the Prophet Elias.

Bluey was already there with three other escapees. They were half-dressed and crouched near the windows, shivering in the night air. Bluey's fists clenched a long rifle.

The five of them huddled together, worried by the sounds of their own breathing and Bluey's belching.

It became deathly quiet.

"I say we break for it now," Bluey whispered.

"Stay put," Mike ordered. "They may be waiting for us."

They looked at each other in puzzlement. "Do what you damned please," Mike said, "I'm riding it out."

He sank into a sitting position with his back against the wall and rubbed his eyes. The empty church looked eerie in the flickering light of the candles burning at the altar at the opposite end.

Bluey grabbed Mike's shoulders and pointed out of the window. Mike's heart pounded as he heard dim, angry guttural commands drift up from the village. It was pitch black, impossible to see anything—only the sounds . . .

Drowsy Greek voices—some angry—some filled with fear—more curt commands in German . . .

"They must be roundin' up everyone," Bluey whispered, trying hard to suppress his nervous burps.

Sounds of motors, trucks rolling into the village. A rifle shot! Angry Greek voices! More rifle shots! The loud wailing of a woman. Mike could swear it was Melpo.

Silence.

Truck motors—one by one—moving away from the village. Motor sounds drifting into silence. No more sounds of Greek voices—only German voices.

An infinitesimal sound caught the ears of the five men. Mike's pistol came from his belt as he squinted desperately into the darkness.

A form—a shadow outside . . . Mike pointed and Bluey nodded in agreement as he lowered his rifle.

The shadow moved unevenly up the path toward the church. Bluey's face was wet with sweat.

Footsteps—slow—half-staggering. The shadow grew larger and larger. The shadow caromed through the window and over the walls of the church. Mike raised his pistol.

The shadow snapped from sight. The five men cowered against the wall, their weapons turned on the door. It burst open.

"Eleftheria!"

She stood there gasping, dressed only in a skirt and blouse thrown on hastily. Mike saw her face by the candlelight—twisted in terror. She was unable to speak.

"Christos," he said. He tore the rifle from Bluey's hands and ran for the door. The four other men pounced on him and wrestled him to the floor.

"You bloody fool! You'll give us all away!"

Mike's grasp on the rifle loosened. He gritted his teeth and beat his fist on the wall, then half-staggered to a bench and slumped onto it.

A gush of wind whipped through the church and the flames at the altar danced crazily and lashed weird shadows over the walls.

He looked up at Eleftheria. Her eyes were those of a crazy woman's. She slid along the wall toward the door. Mike sprang from the bench and grabbed her arm. She screamed hysterically and sunk her teeth into his hand.

German boots coming up the path!

Mike shook her. She opened her mouth to shriek and struggle free. His fist lashed out and thudded against the side of her face. She slumped unconscious into his arms.

"Split up and get out of here!" Mike commanded.

He threw the girl over his shoulder and ran the length of the church toward a small window beside the altar. He pushed Eleftheria through and crawled after.

A thundering crash of a rifle butt against the church door!

Mike lifted the girl into his arms and staggered up

the path toward the woods. ... Three hundred yards ... He ducked behind the first row of trees and sank to his knees and lowered Eleftheria to the ground. He rubbed the numbness from his arms and fought for breath.

A voice shattered the air. "You bloody Huns! You'll never get Bluey alive!"

A chatter of guns and the voice was still.

Eleftheria stirred on the ground. Her huge eyes snapped open. Mike's hand clamped over her mouth. She shook violently. Mike dragged her to her feet and pulled her through the forest away from the advancing sounds of boots.

Faster—faster—faster—the brush ripped their clothes and tore into their skins—faster—faster—away from the flashlights—the barking dogs—the commands . . .

The sound of the Germans grew dimmer and dimmer. Mike clutched at a tree in a dizzy sweat. Eleftheria fell to the ground, sobbing. She rolled over on the dirt, writhing in anguish and her hands tore at her hair and she babbled like a madwoman.

"Get up, you little fool," Mike gasped. "Get up! We—we've got to get away from here. Get up! get up!"

She answered with an hysterical shriek. Mike dragged her to her feet once more and slapped her face again and again until she fell against him weak and mumbling.

He lifted her in his arms and staggered higher into the hills.

When he was no longer able to carry her, he dragged her limp body—one hour—two hours—three . . .

Then he fell to the earth, too exhausted to move. He fell beside her and she lay against him sobbing weakly.

The sky opened and a torrent of rain lashed their torn bodies.

At dawn, Eleftheria and Mike crawled from the brush and walked to a hillside and looked far down on the smoldering ashes of what had once been the village of Paleachora.

SIX

Eleftheria sat on a boulder, too exhausted to speak and too dried out for further tears. There were no words Mike knew or would ever know to comfort the girl. From the barn loft she had seen Christos shot down in the village square while resisting the Germans and she had seen Melpo bayoneted as she knelt over her husband.

During the confusion of the roundup Eleftheria had managed to escape from the barn along with a few other villagers. Mike's escape had been possible only because the bulk of the German force had been concentrating on a roundup of the villagers while the remaining soldiers were scattered tracking down five escapees. In his short stay in Paleachora Mike had learned the lay of the land and the places where the forest was thickest.

The two of them circled about in the hills all day away from the ashes of Paleachora. From their high vantage point they could see German patrols working, fanning out in a growing circle until they gave up futilely at dusk.

The end of the day found Mike and Eleftheria still numbed with disbelief, wet, shivering cold and their bellies rumbling with hunger.

Mike reckoned it was safe enough to risk a small fire. Its warmth revived them. He gathered up several armfuls of pine needles and piled them near the fire, then went to Eleftheria and knelt beside her.

"You'd better get some sleep," he said. "You can start for Dernica in the morning."

She stared down at Mike. Her black eyes were lusterless and rimmed with red. "What will become of you?"

"Don't worry about me. I've caused enough trouble."

"You cannot blame yourself. You did not bring the Germans to Greece."

Small consolation, Mike thought—damned small consolation. Soutar wasn't kidding. Heilser will look behind every rock and every tree. He tried to shake the feeling of inevitable doom, but he couldn't. What chance did he have against this force? How many more times could he be lucky?

Mike put his arm about the girl and led her to the bed of pine needles. She lay down and stretched her tired body. Her blouse had been almost completely ripped by the underbrush. He could see the dark mounds of her breasts and their red pointed nipples.

Her eyes were intent on his. Her hands reached up slowly and drew the blouse apart, baring herself for him to see. She was silent and motionless save for a growing unevenness in her breathing. Mike felt the blood rush through him.

Her breasts rose and fell, and her eyes looked up at him languorously.

He spun around. "I'll get some more pine needles to

cover you. It's going to be cold." He stacked several armfuls of needles over her and built up the fire. For several moments he pondered, then fixed another bed on the other side of the fire.

The sun fell in a few moments.

Mike rolled close to the fire and tried to shut out all thought of the girl on the other side. It turned dark. He could hear her thrash about restlessly.

It seemed fantastic to him that he would want to take her at a time like this. Perhaps it was his feeling of utter defeat that prodded him to seize a moment of joy. I'm not one of these noble bastards, Mike told himself. What the hell's the matter with me?

He knew the answer. Eleftheria wasn't the kind one could be casual with. No—she'd end up with a broken heart and he'd end up with a messy conscience. He turned his back to the fire and shut his eyes. He would not have slept except for the total exhaustion.

But the sleep was tormented. Once again he ran down the list of names—the cursed names—the seventeen names—and Stergiou and Soutar and Christos dressed in his *funstanella* and blood all over his white skirt and Melpo wailing over him. And flames—flames dancing high and licking cruelly at the little white cottages and German soldiers dancing around the flames—dancing the *calamatiano* and the fire burned higher and higher.

Mike opened his eyes and sighed with relief.

The forest was still and dark.

It was freezing cold; the fire was a mass of smoldering embers. He sat up and rubbed his legs and crawled away groping for more wood.

"Jay?" Eleftheria's frightened voice called out.

"I'm here. Go back to sleep."

He knelt beside her and put some fresh twigs on the fire. In a moment they were crackling.

"I am cold," she said.

"It will warm up in a couple of minutes."

He crawled back beneath his blanket of pine needles and stretched out on his back.

"Jay?"

"What do you want?"

"I am frightened."

He hesitated for a long while. "Well—all right, come on over here."

His heart pounded as he heard her stir and felt her slip beside him timidly. "Poor kid, you're just like ice." He rubbed her arms and shoulders and she purred like a kitten as the warmth returned to them. She pressed close to him and his hand reached into her blouse and against the soft satin flesh of her back. Her head nestled on his chest and her arms folded tight around him.

"S'agapo," she whispered.

"Sleep, honey . . ."

"S'agapo," she said and closed her eyes.

A warming ray of sunlight found its way through the trees into the clearing. Mike opened his eyes. The fire was dead. He slipped his arms from Eleftheria, arose, stretched and patted his empty belly. The sun felt good and his mood was a bit more on the optimistic side.

The girl rolled over on her back and squirmed. Mike caught himself staring at the rip in her blouse. He turned away to find more kindling as Eleftheria opened her eyes and looked about and propped up on an elbow.

She tossed her long black hair onto her shoulders with a little flip of the head and made a sweet picture as she encircled her knees and rested a cheek on them. She stared at Mike and smiled as he reset the fire. She looked young and fresh and lovely—and eager.

Suddenly, Mike crushed his lips on hers and her body arched against his and they fell to the earth clutching each other. His hand groped for her breast— and ripped the blouse from her. He felt the sweet pain of her teeth tearing into his shoulder and her fingers clawing his back.

Eleftheria was a little savage. Mike's fingers became entwined in her hair and he drew her face back. Her black eyes flamed with passion and her body pulsated with the fury of a tigress. They were on the ground again, rolling and thrashing about wildly and their lips sought each other out in mounting violence.

Mike strained every fiber in his body as he shoved her away and staggered to his feet. Eleftheria clung to his waist. He grabbed her hair and flung her away. She lay there, her fingers clawing at the earth, panting in her access of passion.

Mike gasped for air as he looked down in puzzled anger at the half-naked girl. He peeled his shirt off and threw it to her.

"Put this on!"

"Please—darling . . ."

"We've got enough goddamned trouble! Put this on!"

The sharpness of his command startled her into submission. In an instant she sank back to her natural shyness, and obeyed.

An hour passed before either of them spoke. But in the silence everything was said that needed to be said.

"You'd better get started for your village," he spoke at last.

"And where will you go?"

"Athens. I'll get there somehow," he answered—not even convincing himself.

"You can never get to Athens alone—you know that. You must come to Dernica with me."

"And see another village get burned."

"You cannot take the blame—you cannot . . ."

"What's the difference . . . ?"

"I will not leave you," she said softly.

Mike knew he could not rove the hills indefinitely. He knew he could not go to Dernica. He knew he could not get to Athens, nor could he afford to cut off from the girl. He further knew that no place in Greece would be safe for long from the relentless Konrad Heilser.

"I have a distant cousin, Despo, who lives in Kaloghriani," Eleftheria said. "It is many kilometers away in the hills. You will be safe there."

"No," Mike said. "I must get to Athens."

"The village is so remote that the Germans do not even know it exists. Then I will help you get to Athens. Come, we can reach it by sundown of tomorrow if we keep going."

SEVEN

Night fell on a pair of weary travelers who felt as though they had reached the end of the world.

They stood five hundred meters above sea level and looked down upon fifty whitewashed cottages which lay in the midst of rocky, barren, eroded hills—Kaloghriani. Below them they could see fragments of the plain near Dadi airdrome and the peak of Mount Kallidromon. The village of Kaloghriani and the land around it were as poor as they were remote.

Eleftheria knocked at the door of a cottage. It swung open and a giant of a man loomed over them. A massive black beard gave him a likeness to the famous portrait of the angry John Brown.

"Kalosorisate!" he roared in welcome when he recognized Eleftheria and ushered them through the narrow doorway into a humble room. "Despo!" he called to his wife. "It is Eleftheria. . . . Bring krasi . . . Hurry, woman!"

A flat homely old woman hurried in from the kitchen and welcomed Eleftheria. Mike, shirtless, stood about self-consciously, as the three exchanged greetings. At last Eleftheria turned to him.

"This is Jay Linden. He is a soldier of New Zealand and he needs a place to stay."

"Englezos?" the giant inquired.

"Yes."

The giant was introduced to Mike as Barba-Leonidas and shook his hand with such violence that Mike thought he would tear his arm from its socket. Barba-Leonidas found a shirt for Mike many sizes too large and then inquired if they were hungry.

In a moment they were seated on backless stools and, without ceremony, Barba-Leonidas dunked his bread into a bowl of lentils and motioned his two starving guests to follow suit.

After the meal, Barba-Leonidas listened intently as Eleftheria unfolded the story of Paleachora. He sat in silent anger broken by an occasional gruff exclamation. Despo, the wife, sat removed from the table at a homemade spindle and did not enter into the conversation.

When Eleftheria had finished, Barba-Leonidas announced, "My only son, Yani, was killed fighting the Italians in Albania. You may have his bed for as long as you wish."

There was something about the direct simplicity of the man that appealed to Mike. He was "real people"— like the longshoremen, the teamsters, the bartenders and the hookers who filled the pages of Mike's books. A quick bond was established between the two.

Dispensing with the social amenities, Barba-Leonidas said, "You are very tired. Go to sleep and we will leave talk for a later time." Then he ordered Despo to find Eleftheria a place to sleep in another cottage. There were but two beds and, as a matter of custom and fact, Mike took priority over a mere woman.

"The one bed will be fine for us," Eleftheria said.

A stunned silence fell on the room. Barba-Leonidas threw an inquiring glance at Mike who had a stupid expression on his face. Barba-Leonidas grunted a few times and looked back and forth from Mike to Eleftheria. Mike just shrugged. The giant continued to mumble to himself, weighing a decision.

"It would not be in proper taste," he declared, and Mike sighed with relief. He did not look forward to another tussle with his conscience.

Mike noticed throughout the evening that Barba-Leonidas became annoyed by the most trifling attention he gave the girl, whether he touched her hand or gave her so much as a small smile. The breed of hill men was obviously more strict about the social status of the female than the men in the village of Paleachora.

Mike walked her to the door where Despo waited. "I'll talk to you in the morning, early. We've got a lot to work out," he said.

The night's restful sleep in the soft down bed worked wonders on Mike's tired bones. He sat down hungrily to the dawn meal with Barba-Leonidas and awaited the arrival of Eleftheria. His mind was filled with plans to get to Athens. The giant remained silent except for his slurping of the boiling-hot coffee. As the meal drew to a close a feeling of alarm swept over Mike.

"Where is Eleftheria?" he asked.

"She went back to Dernica."

"What do you mean she went back to Dernica? Did you send her?"

"She went back. What difference does it make why she went? She went."

"It makes a lot of difference to me!"

"Finish your coffee. It will get cold."

"But . . ."

"Don't get excited. She promises to return on the Sabbath."

Before Mike could argue further, Barba-Leonidas walked out toward the fields. He turned to Despo, who remained as silent as a dumb woman.

Mike grunted angrily. Whose work was this? Was Eleftheria trying to trap him and keep him in this remote place or did the giant send her away for some reason? He didn't like it at all, but there was little choice except to ride it out till the Sabbath and see. He finished his coffee.

Barba-Leonidas was astounded when he looked up from his work in the field and saw Mike standing over him.

"Anything I can do?" Mike asked.

"Bah!" the giant roared in his normal voice. "Go pick grapes with my old woman. I have to clear rocks and I would not want my Englezos friend to soil his tender hands." Mike accepted the challenge and went to work beside him. Barba-Leonidas's fine broad face was a smile from ear to ear.

Yes, Kaloghriani was the end of the world. It was as far removed from civilization as the moon. Mike worked shoulder to shoulder with his host but found it difficult to keep up with the human bear even though he was thirty years younger. They sweated together in the fields during the day and at night they got drunk together. In just three days the bond between them became irrevocable.

Barba-Leonidas found it great sport to tease Mike as the frail little Englezos fellow. Mike was hardly a small man and once was considered a pretty good football player at Cal. They would sneak up on one another and throw wrestling holds. Mike managed to hold his own for a short time—until Leonidas got weary of playing. He would then lift Mike above his head, balance him with one hand and casually flip him into the nearest brush and they would both roar with laughter. Mike often thought of what Cal's team would have been like with seven men like Leonidas on the line. Although he worked hard and drank hard, Mike had never before had the wonderful, joyous feeling of just being alive as he did in his first few days in Kaloghriani.

Despo, the wrinkled old specimen in her drab black homespun and her one tooth hanging lonesomely from her upper gum, was never at rest. Her prune-skinned hands were in constant motion—alongside her husband in the fields, endless housework, gardening the vegetable plot, tending chickens, churning, searching firewood, spinning thread and weaving cloth. She was at work many hours before the sun rose until many hours after it set.

Each day after working the stony, unfertile land the two men would trudge in to the coffee house. There was no song here. Weary men gathered to sit and drink *ouzo* until the simple meal of bread and lentils was ready at home. There were none of the luxuries here that were found in Paleachora.

Yet here, too, Mike found the quality of generosity. As remote as Kaloghriani was, it was not too remote for hungry men to find. Now and then a stray from the desperate cities would show up in search of food. No man left the village without some wheat, either sold at a fair price or simply given away. On the Sabbath Barba-Leonidas and the other men of the village hunted rabbits to feed those who might venture in. There was none of the venality here that was making other farmers rich. The philosophy was simple. If there are two grains of wheat, one should be shared.

And Michael Morrison learned the legend of the place, a legend as ancient as its hills. He was in "the Village of Thieves . . ."

For centuries they had tried to scratch a living from the unyielding land and a boy of Kaloghriani growing into manhood learned it was far easier to exist by looting neighboring villages. So, over the years, the men perfected many daring and unique methods of raiding other villages. The sight of a man from Kaloghriani was unwelcome in the entire province. Thievery became an art and a part of the village culture. There was hardly an adult male who didn't have a prison record.

The village elder, a ninety-nine-year-old named Petros, had spent forty of his years behind bars. Barba-Leonidas bashfully admitted to a few five-year stretches in his younger days—before he mastered his art. The crime was not the stealing but the getting caught. But once caught, a man gained stature in the community by the number of years he spent in prison. And to achieve Averof Prison in Athens—that was the supreme accomplishment. Even Father Gregorios, the priest and only literate person in Kaloghriani, was very vague about ten years he had spent in Canada.

This fantastic breed of hill men must surely have been descendants of the ancient Greek gods, for Barba-Leonidas was a small man among them. Several towered to seven feet and over in height and they lived to be eighty and ninety without a trace of serious illness.

Mike would see them shoot a running rabbit at four hundred yards. Although he was able to work alongside the sixty-five-year-old Barba-Leonidas, he made the sad mistake of trying to outhike him on the day before the Sabbath. The men of Kaloghriani could walk the clock around at a never slackening pace and they could walk uphill as fast as they did downhill, without so much as drawing a deep breath.

The women labored from dusk to dark and were as fiercely rugged as their men, but their beauty faded early. When a child was born, only a few moments after the mother left off working in the field, there was no celebration, no joy. For all things in Kaloghriani—life, death, marriage, disaster—came only as part of another day of work as the Lord doled it out. There was too much to be done for survival to indulge in song or dance or tears.

And so, at the end of the fifth day of Mike's stay, Barba-Leonidas announced in a very matter of fact way that Mike was his son. "My other son was killed" (a matter of little concern, for life went on) "and God has brought me another."

There was little Mike could do to dissuade him from this simple logic.

"Bah! If the Allies are winning the war, why do they retreat? Answer that! Why do they retreat? You are stupid, you stupid Englezos."

"Now don't forget, most of the free world is not yet in the war."

"Bah! If you win, you go forward—if you lose you go backward. The Allies go backward, they lose!"

"Try to get it through your thick skull, Leonidas, the farther the Germans extend their battle fronts the more difficult they become to supply, and the thinner they spread their forces. Look at Napoleon's march on Moscow, for example, in 1812."

"I say, bah! bah! bah! You talk like a woman. If I fight for Kaloghriani and leave it and run to Dadi, I lose—yes or no—yes or no!"

"Aw, for Christ's sake, Leonidas—pour me another glass."

The Sabbath came. Mike awoke early and anxiously awaited the arrival of Eleftheria. By mid-morning his anxiety changed to suspicion. Barba-Leonidas became strangely silent. All during the week he had noticed annoyance every time he mentioned the girl to Leonidas. By afternoon he knew full well that one of two things had happened. Eleftheria was going to see that he stayed in Kaloghriani or Barba-Leonidas was going to see to it.

In the early afternoon Mike had reached the breaking point and demanded to know what was going on. Barba-Leonidas, who could not lie with a straight face, refused to answer. He selected a rifle and stomped from the cottage, announcing that he was going rabbit hunting.

Mike turned to Despo. The aged, wrinkled woman looked up sheepishly from her weaving.

"Eleftheria—where is she?"

Despo shook her head.

"Where is she, dammit!"

Mike stood over her. "Dammit! Tell me where she is!"

"She was here!" Despo cried. "She was here in mid-week. You were in the fields. Barba-Leonidas sent her away."

"Why?"

"Because you are his son and you can never leave."

EIGHT

Mike fumed about the cottage for fifteen minutes. Despo sank back into silence, but her hands nearly flew in nervousness over the weaving machine. Barba-Leonidas had him trapped. He had no way of getting to Dernica—did not even know its general direction. He realized, too, that he'd never get the information from anyone in Kaloghriani. This attempt at fatherhood by the giant was a major problem. Mike had only one choice—to find Leonidas and have it out.

He stormed from the cottage in search of the hunting party. But, given a fifteen-minute lead, it would be almost impossible to find them. They walked nearly as fast as he could run.

Mike traveled away from the village in the general direction of their hunts. For over a half hour he ran about searching vainly. He passed the outermost fields and went into the underbrush. Then, as the land began to rise at the base of Mount Kallidromon, Mike stopped and realized he would have to wait for the hunt to end.

The day was warm and sun-filled and the air was calm and Mike did not feel like spending it in the cottage with the dismal Despo. During the week he had looked up many times from the fields to the mountain and imagined the view was splendid from its peak, so he began to climb.

He started briskly up a time-worn path along one of the slopes and stopped at intervals for a sip of cool spring water and to catch his breath and bearings.

He climbed till afternoon when the mountain began to grow steeper. Mike worked his way to a balding shoulder near the top, crossed a rocky field, and there the peak loomed but a few hundred yards up a sheer wall.

It was strange to Mike. He had always had a dread of heights but now he felt no fear. It seemed as though many fears had vanished in Paleachora and Kaloghri-ani. He tingled with excitement as he edged his way up the wall toward the top.

A breathtaking sight burst below him as he stood atop the mountain with the thrill of a conqueror. To the east the blue Aegean Sea and her islands and to the west the rippling regiments of hills. He stood for many moments electrified by what his eyes saw and a wonderful feeling swept through him. A cloud passed below and disappeared like a ghost into the mountainside and reappeared on the other side. . . .

Mike stood and looked—and wondered. What was the strange power that had brought him to all this? Who was it that wanted him to see it? What was the hunger he had carried all his life that was no longer a hunger?

He thought of his children. At first their images passing through his mind had tortured him. Then they had begun to fade as the days passed. They became distant and lost shape and became foreign. He knew he loved them above all, but he knew too that his mind had adjusted to their loss.

Now he saw seventeen men at elegant desks, or working at files, or attending cocktail parties or hob-nobbing with German officers. The British were probably desperate for these seventeen names. Had he failed? Or had he done right? Perhaps he had been overcautious in wasting weeks. He didn't know. But leave the hills he must. Bullying Leonidas would be no simple chore. Only yesterday Leonidas led the village in burning a German order for wheat allotment.

The only clear plan he could formulate would be to send Eleftheria to Athens to contact Dr. Harry Thackery. Even this was a bad risk. She wasn't the world's brightest and if there was any trouble she'd never be able to cope with it.

Do I have the right to make a pawn of her—risk her life? he asked himself. Many people have already died because of the Stergiou list. Life was a small thing in the struggle to find the names. Then, Mike argued with himself, Eleftheria would want to go to Athens if she knew what was at stake.

One cold fact remained. Her life or his was unimportant in the ultimate delivery of the seventeen names.

Mike took one last look at the view and started down the mountainside.

It was dark when he reached the cottage. Barba-Leonidas was pale when Mike entered. Then, upon seeing Mike, his face broke into an expression of relief which belied his effort to pretend he was unconcerned.

"You stupid Englezos. I was about to go out and look for you. Do not go roaming the hills without me in the future." The giant sat down for his meal. Mike stood over him.

"Tomorrow you go to Dernica and get Eleftheria."

"Sit down and eat and don't talk so much."

Mike grabbed Leonidas by the shirt and lifted his two hundred and fifty pound hulk from the chair. "You go to Dernica or I go."

Barba-Leonidas looked to Despo and shrugged. "Mad—he's gone mad."

Despo edged toward the door, ready to leap out.

"Sit down and eat, I say. If you need a woman that bad, I get you one after dinner. I get you a dozen, take your choice—you can even use my bed."

Leonidas sat and dunked his bread in the bowl of lentils then slurped it into his mouth.

"All right, then. I'm going—right now."

He looked up slowly and stared at Mike with an expression of hurt written all over his bearded face. "What is the matter with you, Jay?"

"Believe me, my friend, I have great love for you, but I must get to Athens."

Leonidas fiddled with his bread, then flipped it down and scratched his beard. "You—you want to leave? You really want to leave?"

"I must leave."

"Why you talk so crazy?" the giant said in a half cry. "Why must you leave?"

"I'm a soldier. It is my duty."

"Bah! What kind of a soldier are you? What you think you are going to do? You can't hit a rabbit at fifty meters with my best Englezos rifle."

"I've seen one village burned to the ground because of me."

"So they burn this stable down. I and my old woman

will live in the bushes. We have done so before, many times. I sometimes think I was happier than trying to raise wheat in these rocks. No, Jay, better you stay with us always."

Mike walked slowly to the little table beside his bed and picked up his possessions. Two pipes, two pistols and the roll of drachmas. He peeled off a million drachmas for himself and set the rest on the table for Leonidas then walked toward the door.

Leonidas arose from the table and blocked him.

"Sit down!" he roared.

Despo knew that tone and fled the cottage.

"You're in my way, Leonidas. Don't make me hit you."

"Sit down or I kill you."

Leonidas rushed to the fireplace and lifted a huge poker and stood before the door and his mouth poured rage. Mike slowly lifted the pistol from his belt and leveled it.

Outside the cottage, the village assembled. A delegation rapped on the door and requested that the pair of them shut up.

For many moments the two men stared at each other. At last, Leonidas turned and threw the poker to the floor. "Like my own son," he mumbled. "How far will you get, Jay? Have you ever seen a blond Greek come from these hills?"

Mike did not answer.

Despo, who rarely showed any emotion of any sort, had re-entered and she wept openly.

"Leave the room!" Leonidas commanded.

He turned to Mike at last. For the first time Mike saw traces of age and weariness. The giant's shoulders stooped and he heaved a sigh through his coarse beard.

"Sit down and eat, Jay. I go to Dernica as soon as I have time."

"When?"

"All right—I go tomorrow."

NINE

Eleftheria felt terribly ill-at-ease in her new city dress and city makeup as she stood in the inspection line at the Larissis Terminal in Athens. Before and behind her were tired city people returning from their scouring of the countryside in search of food.

Her fingers toyed nervously at the latch of the new purse as the line crept toward the desks where German, Italian and Greek inspectors examined travel passes and the sacks and cases the travelers carried.

At last she came before the inspector's desk. A German in civilian attire. She placed her travel pass before him. He looked up and stared at her. She was a pleasant change from those coming through and his look was more in lust than curiosity. Eleftheria avoided his eyes.

"Your business!" he said sharply.

"I visit relatives," she answered almost inaudibly.

He motioned for her purse and turned its contents over on the table. Among other things, a large roll of drachmas fell out.

"This is quite a sum of money."

She did not answer.

"Your occupation?"

"I am the wife of a farmer."

"It seems that all you farmers are coming to Athens with fortunes these days."

She worked hard at containing the uneasiness that flooded her.

"Open your travel bag," the inspector demanded.

He poked through it. It was largely filled with undergarments and other types of things city girls wore. She had purchased them in Dadi as Jay had told her to do.

"You may close it."

He handed the travel pass back and looked wearily down the long line of travelers yet to pass his station. He lit a cigarette and smiled at the girl. "And where will you be staying in Athens, young lady?"

She paused for several seconds.

"I stay with my aunt."

"And—uh—how would you like to see the city with me?"

"My husband waits for me at my aunt's."

"Pass on! Next!"

She walked through the crowded terminal reading the many directions signs. It was all very strange and exciting and frightening. Eleftheria had been to the capital but once before and that was many years ago. Her anxiety threw a ring of solemnity about her that warded off the many amorous glances she was getting from German and Italian soldiers.

She stepped outside and looked around. A long line of taxicabs stood in wait. She took one.

As the taxi moved out, Eleftheria feigned indifference to all the amazing things that were happening. The big city and the many buildings—the car she was riding in. She had been in an automobile only three times before in her life—although she had had several rides in her Uncle Christos' truck.

"I would like you to take me to the American Archeological Society," she said.

The cab wove away from the congestion around the terminal and raced due east across town on the broad Leophoros Alexandrou. She tried to relax and remember the many instructions Jay had given her. She must carry out the job to perfection, she thought.

After several moments they made a right turn and drove alongside a wooded area that went through the northern portion of the plush Kolonaki section.

The cab drove slowly past many buildings, the American hospital, the former British schools and a network of other institutions. On the fringe of these buildings the cab came to a halt. It faced an ordinary-looking two-storied red brick building.

The driver had seemed irritated by Eleftheria's uncommunicativeness during the drive but his face broke into a smile over her generous tip. Anyone connected with the Americans always tipped well.

The cab pulled away. Eleftheria bit her lip. She faced an iron gate that was locked across the driveway. Her heart pounded. She saw an open entrance, a short path leading to the house. She moved toward it with the feeling that she was walking on hot coals.

She pushed open the mammoth door and stood in a reception room filled with statues and paintings and odd bits of marble. There were many framed documents on the walls that she could not read. The room was large and airy and dark and stiff and added to her discomfort.

A middle-aged woman, obviously not Greek, sat behind a small counter with earphones on her head. There was a desk and many papers scattered on it. Eleftheria approached with great caution. The woman looked up and asked, "May I help you?"

"I—I wish to see Dr. Harry Thackery," she whispered.

"Your name, please?"

"My name is Eleftheria."

"Eleftheria what?"

"Eleftheria Yalouris."

"Do you have an appointment with the doctor?" the woman asked, looking inquiringly at the uncomfortable peasant girl before her.

"No. He does not know me."

"Just a moment, please," the woman said. She rose from behind the counter and disappeared behind a large double door that led down a long corridor. Eleftheria thought it strange that a woman could sit in this room and smoke a cigarette—but so many strange things were happening . . .

The receptionist returned.

"I'm sorry. Dr. Thackery cannot see you."

Eleftheria fidgeted with her handbag and shifted her weight several times. Why does this woman look at me so, she thought. She tried to think of what Jay had told her.

"When can I see him?" That was the right thing to say.

"I'm afraid he is very busy. He is preparing an expedition for some diggings."

She remembered that as a small child she had seen some foreign men digging around Dernica. Before the war foreigners always came to dig all over the province. There was always talk of it.

"But—but—I have traveled all the way from Dadi. It is very important."

There was a buzz from the odd box on the desk. The woman stopped the buzz by sticking a piece of metal attached to a cord into the little hole. The door opened and two men who were not Greeks came into the room and sat down and looked at magazines.

The receptionist looked up to see Eleftheria still standing in front of the counter.

"Just what do you want to see Dr. Thackery about?"

"It is a personal matter and one of great importance—and I have come a long way."

The woman shrugged and once again disappeared behind the double doors. She returned. "Follow me, please," she said. The woman marched briskly down the long carpeted hallway past several doors with little brass name plates on them, turned sharply, and opened one and motioned Eleftheria in. She closed the door behind the girl.

The room was in semi-darkness. The long drapes were drawn. The room was stiff and paneled and Victorian. The only light was a small desk lamp. A man sat behind the desk. He looked gaunt and was pasty in complexion. His hair was thinning and his face was bony. He stared at Eleftheria coldly.

"You wish to see me?" his voice said in a monotone.

"You are Dr. Harry Thackery?"

"That is correct."

She bit her nails and thought very hard to relay Jay's exact words.

"A very good friend of mine," she started, trembling, "stays in the house of my cousin. He wishes to come to Athens. He told me that a mututal friend said to come to see you."

"Sit down, girl."

She edged into a stiff mahogany chair in front of his desk and now she could fully see this zombie-like man.

"Where does this friend of yours stay?"

"He stays in Kaloghriani."

"Kaloghriani?"

"Yes. It is a village that is very remote. It is in the province of Larissa."

The man opened his thin lips. "Tell me about this friend of yours."

"He is a British soldier. One from New Zealand."

Thackery's face remained frigid. "You are talking to the wrong person, young lady. If your friend is a British soldier it would be against the law to bring him to Athens. America is not at war with Germany, and I am an American."

"But my friend says..."

"I'm sorry. I can be of no help to you. I would advise you to leave Athens. This sort of thing can get you into a great deal of trouble."

Eleftheria arose, puzzled. She started to walk toward the door then turned, her eyes beginning to well with tears. "But—your mutual friend—a man from Scotland..."

Silence.

Eleftheria felt her flesh crawl under the steady stare from the weird-looking man who sat half-shadowed behind the desk.

"Why does your friend wish to come to Athens?"

She felt a funny dryness in her mouth as she opened her lips to speak. "He told me to tell you he has seventeen excellent reasons why he wishes to come here."

Thackery rose from his chair. "Remain here. I shall return in a moment."

He was not tall and he was not short but his thinness made him appear tall. Eleftheria felt heady and confused and she wanted very badly to get on the train and return to her village and have no more to do with these strange people. She was sorry she had ever come to Athens.

Dr. Harry Thackery stepped across the hall to another office. A man named Thanassis sat with earphones on his head. He stood up when he saw Thackery.

"You heard her," Thackery snapped. "What do you think?"

"It is Morrison, all right," Thanassis answered.

"Thank God he's still alive. I've all but given up hope."

"We need that information desperately," Thanassis said. "What about that girl in there?"

"Are our traveling companions outside?" Thackery asked, referring to the Gestapo who now kept constant watch on his movements.

"They're there, as usual."

"Better order a car. We're going to have to slip that girl out. We can't take the risk of having them pick her up. Have someone contact Lisa to meet us at Papa-Panos'. I'm sending her up to get him immediately."

Part 3

ONE

Lisa Kyriakides listened intently as Dr. Harry Thackery recited the instructions.

Lisa thought the whole mission odd indeed and too shrouded in mystery and unsaid things. It was the first time that Dr. Thackery had withheld any details from her. But Lisa knew, in the very short time that the Underground had formed, that unquestioning discipline was a requisite. She did not question him; at the same time, she didn't like it.

To travel to far-off Larissa to bring down a lone British escapee was too much to swallow. Perhaps he is an officer of high rank or some functionary in the new Underground—perhaps he was no escapee at all, Lisa thought.

Thackery opened his thin lips . . .

"You will leave for Dadi tonight. Once there, a girl named Eleftheria Yalouris will meet you. She will travel with you to a village named Kaloghriani. She will introduce you to a man you will know only as Vassili.

You identify yourself as Helena. You are not to question him."

Lisa nodded and studied his stone face.

"Our people in Dadi will arrange his travel pass, papers and change his appearance. They will pass payoff money on the train he rides. You are to spare nothing in your power to insure his safety. Is that clear?"

"Yes," Lisa whispered.

"Once you arrive in Athens take him to Lazarus' and contact me immediately."

"Very well."

"Are there any questions?"

"I believe I understand everything."

Lisa repeated the instructions and checked her papers and money.

Papa-Panos, the little priest, entered the room. "Come, children," he said. "It is time to eat."

"Yes," Dr. Thackery said. "I'd better eat and get along. I wouldn't want my two German friends to stand outside in the rain too long."

They walked from the room toward the kitchen. Before they entered, Dr. Thackery turned suddenly and faced the woman. "Lisa, you seem upset today. Is anything wrong?"

"Wrong? No—no—of course not."

"One more thing, Lisa. In the event that something goes sour, if capture seems imminent—you are to kill him. He is not to be taken alive by the Germans."

As they entered the kitchen Lisa's mind was spinning a plan furiously. A plan that could save her children—but would make her a traitor to her own people.

Konrad Heilser groaned, sprawling into a sitting position on the couch. His head throbbed. His eyes were bleary and bloodshot. He half-staggered to the huge marble-topped desk and slumped into the big swivel chair. A picture of his plump homely German wife and three plump homely German children stared at him. He shoved the picture into the top drawer of the desk and withdrew an envelope of headache powders.

What a party it had been! But was it worth the agony now? He mixed the powder and drank it down, screwing up his face. Greek headache powders. They can't do anything right.

Zervos, the fat swine, had thrown a four-day orgy to celebrate the acquisition of his new apartment house. Zervos kept a ten-room penthouse, built and furnished in ultra-modern style and hideously scrambled with ancient art works standing alongside surrealist pieces. It was the museum of a madman.

Everyone in the High Command had showed up. Zervos had suddenly become very popular with his gifts and backslapping and coddling and favors. His extortion game against wealthy Greek families had skyrocketed him into a fortune overnight.

Ah! But the whores! Zervos knows his whores, Heilser admitted to himself. A smile crossed Heilser's lips as he remembered the party. A new woman he had found there had turned out very well—much better than the other three.

Then Konrad Heilser's smile turned to a scowl. Zervos, the lout! A scummy government clerk. Zervos was getting too big, too fast. He was currying the favor of everyone with promises of more fabulous parties. Everyone was seeking Zervos now—the fat lout.

He'd lay the law down to Zervos, show the Greek pig who was who. Zervos had promised ten million drachmas a month to Heilser so that he could run his little extortion game. Heilser would demand double that.

But Heilser knew that Zervos had grabbed too much power. He also knew the fat man was too valuable to be disposed of. He had his finger on everything. And there would be ten million drachmas a month coming in. Heilser decided that Zervos would stay, but he'd keep him under control—he'd damned well do that.

Konrad Heilser shuffled through the papers on his desk. Escapees were everywhere. The filthy British roamed the length and breadth of the land. Now there were reports of an Underground movement becoming more active daily.

But this was not the main problem. The main problem was the Greeks working inside the German Command who were pilfering information. Who were they?

Who knew where the American was now? Each day he remained free the threat increased. If the names fell into British hands there would be hell to pay. It would turn his job into a nightmare. There would be no stopping an Underground that knew what the German movements would be. What was the matter with these people? Why did they resist? Only yesterday he had signed an order to destroy two villages in the Aetolo-Acarnania district for harboring escapees and defying wheat taxation. Still they resisted.

Once the American was bagged—once the Stergiou list was known he could set the resistance back two years.

Heilser still felt that Morrison would contact someone in Athens. The German knew who the logical contacts were and he allowed them to operate in the open. It would have been a simple matter to round them up and throw them all into Averof, but he would not do so until he found the American.

A knock on the door. Zervos entered.

Heilser glared at him in disgust. He looked the part of an idiot. His tailor-made suit and vest were of some weird color, and he was fatter than ever. Diamond stick pin, diamond cufflinks, four diamond rings. Soon he'd fill his teeth with diamonds. Zervos walked up to Heilser's desk without a trace of the old fear.

"We have an appointment to meet Lisa Kyriakides in an hour, Konrad." Zervos gloried in the newly found equality which allowed him to call Heilser by his Christian name.

Heilser was repelled, and reminded himself to talk to the Greek swine soon about his come-uppance.

Zervos knew about the personal interest the German had in Lisa, and he goaded, "Well, Konrad"—with a mocking sigh—"I think it is about time we dispose of her."

"I still run this department, Mr. Zervos. So long as there is a chance that one of these people will lead us to Morrison, we cannot dispose of them."

"But in Lisa's case," Zervos continued, "she will not give information. You know that. It is foolish to allow her to run around free. The least we could do is put a watch on her."

"You idiot! Put a watch on her and the Underground would know it in five minutes. No, Zervos, she will obey us as long as we hold her children."

Zervos continued needling the angered German. "Why don't we just have one of the children disappear? That would bring her to her senses. I'm *sure* she'd co-operate more fully if one of her children disappeared."

Heilser knew that was a sensible thing to do. But it would also destroy any chance of her becoming his

mistress. The thought of her was constant and torment-
ing.

Zervos smiled and offered him a cigarette. "You are
being quite unreasonable, Konrad. I have already
offered her fifty million drachmas to—uh—share my
apartment. She is a very, very difficult woman."

"Shut up!"

TWO

Lisa Kyriakides walked across Constitution Square
toward the row of shops facing it on Hermes Street.
Men—Greek, German and Italian—all turned and
watched her pass. She looked straight ahead, neither
ignoring nor acknowledging the stares that followed
her. For Lisa had been endowed with a striking beauty
that could impress itself on a memory even if seen only
as a face in a passing crowd.

The lines of her face were carved to perfection and
set in a halo of golden hair—rare for a Greek. Her
complexion was a shade lighter olive than most
Greeks'. She moved along Hermes Street with the grace
and carriage of a noblewoman.

Lisa was thin, a bit too thin. But this seemed to add
to her haunting loveliness. Her eyes had an expression
of deep sadness. Her hands, almost too sculptured to be
real, seemed to express emotion even as she walked.

Lisa came to a halt before the window of Anton's
Dress Shop. Anton, the pseudo-Frenchman, who

guaranteed his high-paying clientele the latest fashions from Paris.

A German officer approached her dubiously, hoping to introduce himself. Lisa cut him with an icy stare that sent him scurrying across the street.

She drew a deep breath, tightened her lips to hold off the tears, then opened the door to Anton's and stepped into the deeply carpeted reception room.

Anton, dressed in stripes and cutaway, met her and bowed from the waist in recognition. She followed him past the ornate showroom where soft music accompanied a model parading before a customer. They turned into a long corridor past fitting and sewing rooms and into his office.

"Kindly be seated," Anton said in his high-pitched voice. "They will be here shortly." He bowed again and departed.

Lisa sank into the leather couch and buried her face in her hands. Tears fell down her proud cheeks. In a moment she braced herself and walked to the liquor cabinet for a brandy.

She stared blankly at the painted wall.

What was there left to live for?

It started the day after the German entrance into Athens. Manolis Kyriakides, her husband and the father of her two children, had showed his true colors.

Lisa's father, a small factory owner, had defiantly refused to do business with the Germans. He had destroyed many patents the enemy sought.

This was what Manolis had been waiting for. Waiting since the day he had married Lisa. Within a week, Manolis gained control of the factory as the prize for collaboration with the Germans. It was Manolis' information that sent Lisa's father to Averof Prison. The old man lived only a few weeks, refusing to divulge the patents up to the moment of his death.

A week after her father's passing, Lisa learned the true story from a friend. At first, Manolis tried to deny his part. But Lisa knew the truth. Long ago she had learned his pattern of greed and ambition.

She took the children and left him and went into hiding in an apartment in Athens. Then she became one of the first to join the new Underground movement.

Inside a week, she was picked up by the Gestapo.

Manolis, now deep in the Germans' favor, regained the children. And, so great was the influence of Manolis Kyriakides, the collaborator, that Lisa's life was spared. He took the case up to Herr Heilser himself. Yes, Manolis was a fine man. Not many husbands would do that for a wife who deserted.

But there had been a motive behind Manolis' plea for his wife, just as there had been a motive for every move he had ever made in his life. He knew what would happen when Heilser saw her. It was his calculation that Heilser would become infatuated, as did all men. He knew he would continue in Heilser's favor once Heilser saw his wife.

But Lisa threw a wet blanket on Heilser's idea of acquiring her as a mistress. Yet the German allowed her to live. She would change her mind, sooner or later, and Konrad Heilser was a man of patience and persistence. Lisa would be worth waiting for.

Her capture had been so swift that the Underground was unaware of it. They were unaware she was being forced to report to Zervos and Heilser. Zervos was the one who had concocted the charming scheme of holding her children as hostages.

It all buzzed around Lisa's head like a hideous nightmare. At first she thought of suicide. But suicide would have endangered the lives of her children. Manolis was bound to outsmart himself sooner or later and he was too weak to raise a finger to save them. She could not sentence her own sons to death!

But she could not go on playing both sides. Avoiding Heilser's and Zervos' questions. Lying to them. Up to now she had not been followed, but how long would that continue? How long before Konrad Heilser took the life of her children?

And what if her own people learned of her dual role and she died at their hands as a traitor?

There was a way out. . . . Manolis' way out. Become the kept woman of Konrad Heilser. Lisa cringed as she thought of the lustful face of the German.

The black staff Mercedes-Benz stopped in front of Anton's Dress Shop. Heilser and Zervos stepped out flanked by their bodyguards.

Anton bowed low. Zervos reacted favorably to the treatment. After all, Anton did not have many such customers as he.

"Has she arrived?" Heilser asked.

"Yes, sir—yes, sir . . ."

They brushed past the bowing and scraping proprietor and walked down the corridor into the office.

Lisa stood before them like a frozen statue. Heilser's heart missed a beat at the sight of her.

"Well!" he snorted sharply.

"There is nothing to report. I have not been contacted."

"Come now, Lisa," Zervos interjected, "this is the same story you gave us last visit."

"Now, let's stop this lying, Lisa," Heilser said.

"I have told you before, I am contacted each time by

a person who uses a false name. I can never tell where or when I will be reached or for what purpose. I have not been contacted since you released me," she lied. "Perhaps they know I had been taken into custody."

"Stop lying!"

"Do you wish us to bring the head of one of your sons on a plate the next visit?" Zervos barked.

This did not receive the reaction Zervos hoped for. The woman showed no trace of fear. She spoke in an unwavering voice. "I intend to keep my bargain as long as you keep yours."

The pair were stopped cold in the face of Lisa's courage and calm.

"Wait outside," Heilser ordered Zervos.

The German paced back and forth, then seated himself at Anton's desk and gave her his most charming smile. Lisa remained frozen.

"My dear," Heilser cooed, "you are making things extremely difficult for yourself and without reason. I would like to believe your story, Lisa, sincerely, I would. I have not put guards on you—I said I wouldn't, didn't I?"

She did not answer.

"Lisa—dear. You know I'm trying to help you—protect you."

"I ask nothing. We made a bargain. I shall report to you as long as I'm allowed to see my children."

Heilser sighed and feigned sympathy. "I hope they stay healthy."

Then he got up abruptly. His emotions began to boil at the thought of having her in bed with him. He walked around the desk and stood facing her. Her flesh crawled as he reached out and ran his hands over her shoulders and in her hair and over her cheeks. His jaw trembled as he tried to speak. "Lisa—I'll—I'll do anything . . ." He seized her and buried his lips in her neck.

She remained absolutely frigid.

He drew back and looked into her eyes, pleading. Her answer was a look filled with hatred and disgust.

Heilser raised his hand and slapped her cheek. She did not flinch. He spun about and walked from the room, slamming the door behind him.

Lisa closed her eyes and held the edge of the desk for support. Half in a trance she walked to the window and looked out at the black car rolling away. She knew that time was running out quickly and she had to make her decision.

Then a thought hit her—an avenue of escape. Her mission—the man she was to bring to Athens. He was certainly bound to be of importance to the Germans. Perhaps, without the Underground knowing it, she could allow a slipup. Perhaps she could barter for him with the Germans. If he was important enough, she could make a deal for the return of her children. She would move to another part of Greece. The Underground need never know. . . .

THREE

Eleftheria buried her face in her hands and wept. "I will never see you again," she cried.

Mike knelt by her chair. "Eleftheria," he said softly. "You nursed me when I was sick—you risked your life for me—what can I say? What can I tell you?"

She flung her arms around his neck and drew his head against her bosom. "Take me with you! Take me with you!"

Mike pulled her arms loose. He stood up and turned his back. "Please don't make it any more difficult than it is—please."

"You don't love me," she said.

"It wouldn't make any difference whether I did or not. It wouldn't make any difference."

"You don't love me."

He turned slowly and faced her and shook his head, no.

It was quiet for a long time.

The girl walked to the large open fireplace. Her back stiffened and she held her head high. "I shall return to Dernica. There is a boy there who wants to marry me. He has wanted to marry me since we were . . ." Her voice faltered and tears streamed down her cheeks.

Mike walked up behind her. His hands squeezed her shoulders. He turned and walked quickly from the room.

Barba-Leonidas grumbled as he placed a quarter of a large cheese in the package he was preparing for Mike. He grumbled that he didn't trust women in general and city women in particular.

Old Despo began wailing at her weaving machine.

"Get out of the cottage and cry, old woman!" her husband shouted.

"Two blonds on a trainload of Greeks," he sputtered, tying up the ends of the bundle. "Even the Macaronades aren't that stupid."

Lisa sat quietly as the scene unfolded. The barefooted peasant girl who watched from the doorway was obviously in love. Most likely they had had an affair,

Lisa thought. Eleftheria's eyes, filled with jealousy, glared at Lisa.

"We must be started if we are to reach Dadi by sundown."

Mike nodded.

He took one of his pistols and shoved it into Barba-Leonidas' hamlike hand as a gift. It was the same pistol that had been earmarked for his death by Mosley outside of Kalámai. Once again Mike tried to offer money, but the giant proudly refused.

The two men stood facing each other awkwardly and tears welled in the corners of Leonidas' eyes. He seized Mike in a bear hug. "God be with you," he whispered. He turned and walked from the cottage.

Mike lifted the sack to his back and nodded to Lisa. They walked from the cottage and climbed aboard a donkey cart. In a moment it nudged down a path away from Kaloghriani.

Mike turned around and looked back to the hills. He saw the colossal form of Barba-Leonidas outlined against the sky, and Eleftheria stood at his side. He smiled sadly. "Forgive the hearts and flowers, but they are my friends."

"I understand," Lisa answered in perfect English.

The cart turned onto another dirt path and soon Kaloghriani disappeared completely from their sight.

Lisa glanced at the man she knew as "Vassili." He was not at all as her mind had pictured he would be. He was a strapping, extremely handsome man, deeply tanned, and his beard was close cut and neatly trimmed. His pale-blue eyes had a penetrating and searching look.

His eyes frightened her. Mike had observed her carefully when she entered the cottage but his look was not like that of other men. It was a look of curiosity and it

seemed to penetrate her thoughts. She was uncomfortable in an instant and avoided his glances. Who is
he? she thought. Could he possibly be aware? Could he
possibly know?

Lisa looked at her watch. They could make Dadi by
nightfall, a bit later than anticipated. There were many
things to be done.

It was pleasant here in the hills, far from Athens.
Athens had turned into a city of sorrow. Here, the birds
sang as if they did not know their land had been
conquered and the forest stood tall and proud.

Mike was quiet.

He felt that a door had shut behind him which he
might never be able to open again. He felt he would
never again know men like Barba-Leonidas and Christos and the peasants of Paleachora and Kaloghriani. He
was surprised at how deeply he felt the loss of Eleftheria.

All his life Michael Morrison had accepted mediocrity in people. He accepted it fully when the long struggle
to produce his first book was over and the shocking
disappointment of a small sale embittered him.

He accepted mediocrity when his writing turned sour
and his pages were cluttered with mediocre people. It
had become a struggle to keep at his typewriter and he
had hated himself as he saw his words drip venom.

The death of Ellie had seemed to put a stamp of
mediocrity on him for life.

But now as he came from the hills an urge to write
again overwhelmed him—to write about wonderful,
beautiful people he never knew existed. People who
faced crushing tragedy not with defeatism, but with
hope. People whose lives were uncluttered and warm.
He had found the secret of the true nobility of man in

these hills and he wanted to reveal it in the only way he knew how—at his typewriter.

The day was a long and silent one, both of them withdrawn in their own thoughts.

At nightfall the donkey cart pulled into the town of Dadi.

Mike and Lisa were shaken from their reveries.

For Mike, it was as though he was coming into another age. He was intrigued by the red-tile roofs, by the sight of an automobile and a sidewalk, to say nothing of the women in modern dress.

The donkey driver was dismissed and they set off for the main square. Lisa led Mike to a bakery run by a hefty character identified as Baziadis.

A room in the rear of the bakery turned out to be an arsenal. It had a cache of everything from pistols to homemade bombs and machine guns. A second man, Rigas, a photographer, locked himself in with them and went to work.

First, Mike was given a suit of second-hand city clothes. Rigas photographed him and then presented him with forged travel papers and a card which bore the name: Vassilios Papadopoulos. Then Rigas produced train tickets and money and went over instructions with Lisa.

Baziadis, the bakery owner, came in after his night's baking chores were over, and the four of them joined in a silent meal.

It was two in the morning when everything was declared in order and Rigas and Baziadis left.

Lisa and Mike stretched out on cots at opposite ends of the room. A small bare light bulb burned all night.

It was impossible for Mike to sleep. His head was riddled with questions about the trip.

The woman he knew as Helena was wide-eyed too.

She was indeed a beautiful thing, Mike thought. But there was somthing terribly strange about her, something he could not put his finger on, but something he did not like.

"Do you have a cigarette? I don't want to break the package open for pipe tobacco."

She sat up and opened her purse. As Mike lit up their eyes met. They stared at each other for a long time.

Then Lisa turned her head away and lay back on the cot.

"We'd better get some sleep," she said.

FOUR

Morning.

Both Lisa and Mike showed signs of sleeplessness. They arose, washed in cold water and ate a hasty meal of cheese and milk.

Mike had spent the entire night with his hand on his pistol and his head filled with fears and distrust. The morning found him edgy and taut. He jumped at every strange sound.

About seven o'clock, Baziadis came and opened the bakery and they departed through a rear door. The silence between them continued on the short walk through the square to the railroad depot.

When Mike saw the train pulling in, all his apprehensions took possession of him. As the train neared, it began to take on the shape of a coffin. He again felt for the pistol in his belt, but this time it gave him little comfort.

Lisa held his arm. They walked through the depot shed onto the platform. The wheels ground to a halt. The train hissed. Travelers scurried off and on to calls by the station master.

The pair edged toward a car. Mike halted abruptly.

He saw a conductor standing beside a car exchange glances with Lisa and nod. Lisa nodded back in recognition.

Mike froze, but at her prod he moved on. They stepped into the train.

He looked down the aisle quickly. It was a car of wooden benches, half-filled with city people. All of them were wailing a unanimous chorus of troubles. He scanned the car for a sign of a hostile or alien face. No one gave them a second glance as they found a double seat.

Mike sat beside a window and tried it out. It worked smoothly.

His heart jumped as the train started and moved out of the Dadi depot.

Lisa avoided conversation and even looking at Mike. But she could feel his tension. His hands had been wringing wet when she led him onto the train. She hoped everything would go off on schedule. His nervousness could well upset her whole plan.

She looked past Mike out of the window. Scenery flitted by.

No sooner did the train get up speed when it slowed for another village. Then another—and another. The car became jammed. People sat on their baggage in the aisles. Stop and go—stop and go—stop and go.

Mike managed to relax a trifle. He took out some pipe tobacco and lit up. It smelled good to Lisa. Her father had smoked a pipe of the same sharp-smelling blend and its scent drifted her back into memories of happier days. . . .

The clock pressed toward noon. By now Mike was more at ease but he remained alert. The chorus of misery about them did not lessen for an instant.

Early afternoon.

Lisa became restless. Her energy was drained. Mike reckoned she was not too strong a girl and was probably worn out from the trip up to Kaloghriani.

"You look tired," he said. "Why don't you stretch out over the seat and take a nap?"

She said, "No," in what was an automatic rejection of any male proposal.

"Go on, it will do you good."

Lisa smiled weakly. It was the first time Mike had seen that smile. It was warm and wonderful. She glanced at her watch, then curled up and put her head in his lap, her legs tucked under her. At first she was stiff and aware of him, then she eased and began to doze. In several moments the weariness lulled her to sleep.

Mike gazed down at her. Perhaps he had been wrong. Under the circumstances, it was only natural for him to be keyed up. She was certainly a beautiful woman, although she looked almost childlike sleeping there. A sudden thrill passed through his body. He had an irresistible urge to touch her hair. . . . At that moment, he did not care if the train ever reached Athens.

Then he stretched his legs and tapped out his pipe. In a few moments his eyes shut and the rhythm of the wheels lulled him into an exhausted sleep. Lisa looked up from his lap, now much more at ease that he was asleep.

Three men stood over them.

Mike's eyes opened. He stared at them in fright. He felt a nervous twitch start from the corner of his eye.

One of the men was the conductor, the same one who had exchanged signals with Lisa at the depot.

Next to him, in the crowded aisle, stood two armed men in the uniforms of Italian carabinieri. He felt Lisa stir and knew she was awake but feigning sleep.

"Identification!" one Italian snapped.

Mike began to fumble through his pockets with trembling hands. Lisa came awake quickly.

Her hand reached up to Mike's inside pocket and took out his travel card. She sat up, stretched, yawned and touched her disheveled hair.

"Vassili, you are always misplacing things. I told you to let me hold it," she said, patting Mike's cheek and bussing him softly. She handed the card to the Italian. "Oh, to be married to a teacher at the university! His head is always in the clouds."

Lisa smiled at them, the type of smile a woman uses to lure a man. The Italian was all business. He was not lured.

"Vassili," she said, "give the gentlemen our tickets. Do not keep them waiting."

The carabinieri in their funny Napoleonic hats scrutinized Mike's card. They kept staring from the card to Mike. They began to whisper to each other. Lisa and the Greek conductor's eyes met.

Mike's hand felt for the pistol in his belt. He turned and looked outside. The train was slowing.

"You! Stand up! Open your bundle!"

Mike got to his feet slowly.

"Come on now," the conductor moaned. "The train is full. It will take us all night. Let's get on with it so we may return to our card game."

The Italian read the back of the card, looked up at

Mike again, then handed the pass back and moved to the next seat forward.

The train gathered speed.

It took Mike many moments to calm down. He felt foolish and disgusted with himself. Obviously the woman and the conductor knew what they were doing. He remained rigid until the inspectors left the car.

"Give me a cigarette," he said.

She handed him a pack labeled Number 1.

"I want your pistol," she whispered sharply.

"Nothing doing."

"Stop speaking in English, you fool. People are staring at us. Another stupid move like that and you'll land us both in Averof. Now give it to me; we'll never get off the train with it."

Mike gritted his teeth and fussed like a small boy then reluctantly slipped the pistol to her. He felt naked the instant he was without it. Lisa put it in her purse quickly and made off down the aisle.

In several moments she returned to the seat.

"What did you do with it?"

"It is on the rail bed somewhere between Amphissa and Levadeia."

"You're mad at me, aren't you?"

She was. She didn't answer.

"How much more of this do we have?"

"We will not arrive till early morning."

"Well, you might as well try to catch some more sleep."

"You may sleep if you wish. I'm staying awake," she said, obviously referring to his display of panic.

Lisa snuggled into his arms suddenly and kissed his cheek. In a second he realized the affection was for the benefit of the two Italians who were doubling back through the car.

The balance of the trip was spent in utter silence.

It was four in the morning when the train pulled into Larissa Terminal in Athens.

FIVE

The tram ride ended in a suburb of Athens named Chalandri about six miles from the center of the city. It was, in the main, a truck farm and orchard area.

Lisa led Michael down a path in the direction of a frame house, then swung away from it onto another path that ran through a grove of lemon trees. A small isolated pump house appeared in the midst of the grove.

She opened the door and entered first and lit a kerosene lamp. A smell of mustiness hit them. Even though it was almost midday the pump house was dark; the only opening was a twelve-by-twelve-inch mesh screen near the top. The place had long been out of use as a pump house. There were a pair of cots, a table and a chair on the dirt floor. The table held a lamp and a can of fuel. A dozen books on one of the cots caught Mike's attention.

When the train had arrived in Athens many of the passengers attempted to escape inspection by ducking out of the windows. Most of them were rounded up immediately. Mike and Lisa spent four nerve-racking hours before passing the inspection desks and, when it came, it came without incident.

"Home at last," Mike said, dumping the sack on the table.

Lisa stood before him, as aloof as a statue. "Lazarus who owns this farm is one of our trusted people. He is instructed to keep away from here and make no contact with you. You will report if he makes any intrusions."

"Yes, ma'm."

"A meal will be left outside the door daily after sundown. There is a trench latrine alongside the building. You are to use it only after dark. Under no other circumstances are you to leave this house."

"Anything else?"

"You needn't be smart. You were brought here at a great deal of expense and risk."

"You haven't exactly been a member of the Hellas Welcome Wagon, yourself."

Mike sat on one of the cots and it creaked under his weight. He glanced at the titles of the books . . . Shakespeare, Shaw, Wilde, Goldsmith and a bevy of lesser English playwrights and poets. It was a catholic collection. Another set of small volumes bore the names of Aristotle, Socrates and Plato. "Looks like I'm in for some required reading. You don't happen to own an American Western? I'm strictly a diversionist when it comes to reading. . . ."

Mike's attempt at humor didn't register.

"Turn your back," she ordered.

Mike heard the rustle of silk underthings and quelled a natural inclination to peek.

"You may turn now."

In one hand Lisa held his pistol, in the other, his roll of drachmas. She dropped them on the table. "In the future, try to be more discriminating before pulling a gun."

Mike was completely deflated now.

"When do I see Dr. Thackery?"

"As soon as he is ready to see you."

Mike arose as Lisa started for the door.

"Miss . . ."

She turned.

"Look, Helena or Mrs. Papadopoulos or whatever your name is. I know this has all been a routine thing for you but I want to thank you."

"It isn't necessary."

"I'm afraid it is necessary. When someone does something nice I think they should accept thanks. I can tell you I'm grateful for my life, can't I?"

Lisa smiled and her voice lost some of its coldness. "We have been rude to each other. I suppose it was natural under the circumstances."

"You know something? You're not fooling me for a minute?"

"What do you mean?" she said, half-startled.

"You aren't half as cold as you'd like me to believe. I don't suppose we'll be seeing each other, so thanks again."

"I'm afraid you're not rid of me," she said. "I have been assigned to check here daily."

"Swell . . . See you around . . ."

"My name is Lisa."

"See you around, Lisa."

"Good-bye, Vassili."

The long black Mercedes-Benz staff car turned down Hermes Street in the direction of Anton's Dress Shop.

"Do you really think you are doing the right thing, Konrad?" Zervos asked.

"I believe so. Lisa must surely know by now that her time has run out. She will listen this time."

"I don't like it. She may run back to the Underground with the whole thing."

"And perhaps you have a better idea?"

Zervos shrugged. Heilser and Zervos had learned from questioning the villagers of Paleachora that Morrison had been attempting to get to Athens with the aid of a man named Christos who was killed in the raid. Although Morrison had escaped farther into the hills, both of them were certain he had made or was trying to make contact in Athens. Everything now indicated his contact would be a group revolving around Papa-Panos, Dr. Thackery and a former Greek professor named Thanassis.

Anton ushered them into the office where Lisa waited.

"Good afternoon, Lisa," Heilser said in a gentle voice. "You look tired? Have you been feeling well?"

"I am certain my health is of no concern to you."

"On the contrary. I'm quite concerned. Did you see your children?"

"Yes, I saw them."

Heilser paced the room a moment, then balanced himself on the edge of the desk and fiddled with Anton's letter opener. "Tell me, Lisa. Do you know an American by the name of Dr. Harry Thackery?"

"No . . . Why?"

"Oh, we thought perhaps you did."

"He's working with your Underground. No doubt you'll meet him sooner or later, if you already haven't," Zervos said.

The strange line of questioning threw her off guard.

"How about a priest named Papa-Panos?"

"I know him."

"What do you know?"

"Only what everyone else in Athens knows." Lisa

thought, either the two of them are groping or they are on to something. . . .

"Now, Lisa. The purpose of this is to let you realize that we are not entirely ignorant of what is going on."

"I'm sure you're not," she replied.

"We are also aware of the fact that you've been lying to us. But I'm willing to let that be water under the bridge. What I want to know is whether or not you are willing to begin co-operation."

"I made a bargain . . ."

"Just a minute," Zervos interrupted. "You sound like a broken record. Our patience has run out. You understand what we mean without spelling it out?"

"I understand," she whispered.

"I am going to offer you a proposition, Lisa. In exchange for some information, I will return your children to you and arrange a boat for you to Egypt."

Lisa tried to mask her excitement.

Konrad Heilser opened his billfold and handed her a picture. It was one reproduced from the book jacket of Michael Morrison's *Home Is the Hunter*. She stared at it. . . .

"This man is either in Athens or will be shortly. I will give you three weeks to turn him up. If you don't . . ."

She handed the picture back. "Is that all?"

"That is all."

"You may go first today," Zervos said. "I wish to stay and purchase some dresses."

Lisa walked from the office slowly. The eyes of Heilser and Zervos followed her. The door shut.

"She knows them," Heilser said.

"Difficult to tell about that woman—she masks her emotions so well."

"She cannot mask that commendable trait of mother love . . ."

"By the way, Konrad. Do you really intend letting her go to Egypt with her children?"

"Of course not."

"Come. Let us go to my place. I'll show you my latest who will make you forget even Lisa."

SIX

Much of Lisa's usual calm was gone now. In the quiet of her apartment she paced nervously. A half dozen times she made her decision, only to change it. Each time she made up her mind to rebuff Heilser to the end, the picture on the mantel of her two sons taunted her. How helpless, how little they were . . .

The man, Vassili, spoke more like an American than an Englishman. He was of great importance both to the Gestapo and the Underground. Heilser would have not made the proposition to her unless he was desperate. In their last meeting he made no attempt to persuade her to become his mistress. The man, whoever he was, must hold some great power.

But could she betray her own people? What would life be like then? Dr. Thackery, Papa-Panos and Thanassis were just as desperate to have the man escape from Greece. Yes, her sons would live, but how many other sons would die if she betrayed?

Three weeks to decide . . . three weeks . . .

The picture on the mantel—a boy of two and a boy of four. One with a bright smile on his face and the other held a little stuffed bear. Lisa lit a cigarette and sank into a chair.

Mike had no choice but to get accustomed to the pump house in Chalandri. It was obvious that the final dash from Greece was no simple chore to arrange.

He tried to read but couldn't concentrate. He slept in snatches and waited for darkness, for darkness meant he could step outside the shack for a breath of air.

At midday the sweat poured from him. As the sun blazed hotter it would become stifling and unbearable in the house. Mike would lie flat and motionless, almost passing out from the heat.

He was alert to every sound, from the rustle of a tree to the shuffle of footsteps that came after sundown. At the sound of the footsteps he unfailingly reached for his pistol. The steps would grow louder and louder, then stop in front of the door. A dish of food and a bottle of wine would be left and the footsteps would shuffle away.

Mike couldn't eat much, but the wine would throw him into a blessed fog for a few hours.

All through the night he would pace the dirt floor like a caged animal. The days seemed endless.

One sound outside the pump house made him sigh with relief. The soft, light footsteps of Lisa. It was only human, under these conditions, for him to look forward with renewed eagerness to her nightly visit. And it was only natural for him to spend a great deal of time thinking about her when she was gone. Mike felt that he always would have remembered her even if he had met her under ideal circumstances. There was that deep, haunting sadness in her face that seemed to give her beauty a mysterious aura.

Their visits were friendly. Each day Lisa would be more persuasive in her efforts to gain his complete confidence.

"How is it today, Vassili?"

"Great. I love it here. Do you want to hear me recite *Julius Caesar* forward or Plato's *Republic* backward?"

"Well, now, perhaps this will cheer you up a bit."

She opened a package and produced a razor, some blades and two books: *The Sea Wolf* and *Martin Eden*. Mike didn't have the heart to tell her he'd read the books a half dozen times.

"Wait! There is more! Here is a surprise. Look what I have, Vassili—tobacco."

"Tobacco . . ." But even his pipe did not taste good any more. "Lisa, how much longer do I have to stay here?"

"It is very difficult for Dr. Thackery to move about these days, but it should not be too much longer, Vassili, not too much longer."

Five days passed.

Lisa began to arrive earlier and stay almost to the curfew hour. Each day he awaited her more anxiously than the last. He began to think that much of the duty and routine of her visits were disappearing and that she actually enjoyed being with him.

They would brew a pot of tea or share a bottle of wine and relax and converse. They would talk of books and music. He found her to be intelligent and highly educated. And from her Mike learned more of the tragedy that had befallen Greece.

The country was rapidly degenerating into a state of

moral rot. Most Greeks were bitter in their hatred of the invaders, but there were those—as there always are —who thought it better to do business with the enemy.

One series of sledgehammer blows followed another. The area around Athens had never been self-sustaining in food. Now it was being stripped to the last kernel of wheat by the Germans. Crop taxation was in force and villages and fields were being burned wherever defiance flared up.

The Greeks fought back as best they could, only to see their citizens massacred at the rate of fifty to one. Organized resistance did not yet exist.

Mike realized now how much depended on the seventeen men on the Stergiou list who worked in the inner orbit of the Nazi Command.

The ration allowance dropped to almost starvation level. Black markets were beginning to appear. Jungle law was taking over. Schools closed for lack of attendance and children began to rove the country in packs.

This was only the beginning for Greece.

It was a strange relationship between Mike and Lisa. Mike wanted to say so much, but he had to keep on guard always. He wanted to talk about his children and his writing and about San Francisco. Somehow Lisa seemed to fit with San Francisco.

Perhaps it was the strangeness that attracted them to each other. Then, on the seventh night, she abruptly asked if he had had an affair with Eleftheria. At that instant their relationship changed. Lisa seemed annoyed with herself; then she retreated to her original coldness.

On the eighth day she did not visit him.

The ninth day.

Lisa lifted the phone and dialed Gestapo. Her face was chalky and beads of perspiration formed on her brow. She asked for Zervos.

"Do you know who this is?" she said.

"Yes," Zervos answered.

"Tonight at ten I shall be walking down Æolou Street past the National Bank. I may have someone with me."

"Very well."

Lisa hung up the receiver and clenched her teeth to fight off the uncontrollable tremors in her face.

The door to the shack opened.

Mike smiled as Lisa entered. He was so happy to see her, he was willing to forget yesterday when she did not come.

"I have good news, Vassili," Lisa said. "We are going into Athens tonight. We have made contact with someone about your departure."

SEVEN

They left the pump house.

Mike walked beside Lisa toward the tram line and he was riddled with conflicting feelings. First there was the relief of his departure from the pump house. There was excitement at the thought of getting out of Greece, and there was a little sadness in the knowledge that he'd never see Lisa again. But uppermost in his mind were the same fears that had tormented him before the train ride from Dadi to Athens.

He had seen Lisa operate coldly and efficiently. He had seen her in a warm and friendly mood. But he had never seen her act in doubt. Now she was betraying too many signs of nervousness for his comfort.

The tram rolled into the northwest corner of Athens and continued down a broad road past the large grounds of the Ceramicus.

They got off on October Street and took off afoot in the general direction of Concord Square.

It was eight-thirty.

She held his arm and at that moment much of the doubt vanished. As they strolled he became terribly aware of her nearness.

A feeling came over him that he had not had in many many years. A feeling he thought he'd never have again. His memory telescoped backward in time some eighteen years. Now he was just a fellow with his girl taking a walk, nowhere in particular—just killing a day.

A walk in the flower-filled Golden Gate Park past the concourse where the band played. Or a walk toward the Memorial Stadium in Berkeley in the fresh nip of November air before the big game between Cal and Stanford.

It may have been a week-end hike in the hills of Marin over the Golden Gate Bridge or it may have been a lazy stroll past the sun bathers at Playland at the beach.

There would always be a girl beside him and he would feel good. He felt good now with Lisa beside him and he wondered why this feeling returned after so many years and in this foreign place.

Athens was depressing. Shops that once were bursting with goods were now bare. The people looked emaciated as they ambled lifelessly through the streets.

Sinister-looking Nazis and comic-opera carabinieri replaced the happy-go-lucky khaki-clad British Expeditionary Force. Young girls, now condemned to whoredom, stood back in the shadows.

As the crowd thickened near Concord Square, Lisa suddenly stopped, then changed their direction to a quieter side street.

They seemed to be strolling aimlessly. Lisa checked her watch. It was after nine.

The street was empty.

They could hear the click of their heels as they walked through the Kolonaki section past the Church of Agioi Theodoroi.

Another block brought them to an intersection of Æolou Street. They stopped.

Mike figured that they had bypassed Concord Square and were directly below it. He looked up Æolou Street and in the distance could make out the Cable Office which he had used several times on his arrival in Athens. A bit above that stood the National Bank.

"Where do we go from here?" he asked.

Lisa took her arm from his. "Up Æolou Street," she whispered.

Mike lit his pipe. The glow illuminated her face. Her eyes betrayed her.

"Wait," she said. "There is time yet. Come, I want to show you something."

They crossed Æolou Street and headed in the opposite direction.

"We get a full moon here so seldom," Lisa said.

"One must never leave Greece without seeing the Acropolis by moonlight."

Mike looked down in hushed awe on the sullen city below. The moonlight shed a silver light down the hill to the flickering lights of Athens and to the sea on the west.

He gazed down the south wall and the moonlight appeared eerie on the yellow marble of the Parthenon at his side.

Once Mike had asked himself what was the power that had brought him to Greece. He had asked in the midst of the turmoil and confusion of a retreating army. He knew, even in the chaos, that a reason was to be found somewhere. In large measure the question had been answered. But here, now, was another answer and another meaning. The very soul of his own country was born on this hill.

Mike turned and faced Lisa. As he stared into her sad black eyes he knew that Lisa was an integral part of the tragedy of Greece.

"There isn't any contact and there isn't any boat, is there, Lisa?" he asked softly.

She pressed her slender body to his, clutched his arms and buried her head on his chest as she trembled and wept.

"Hold me, Vassili—hold me—hold me!" she cried, her voice filled with anguish and desperation.

"What is it? Tell me!"

"Just hold me, tightly—please!"

Mike's arms were around her and she sobbed as they crushed against one another. Then she turned and walked away and slumped down on a marble boulder. Her eyes were as lifeless at the city below. "Come, Vassili," she said softly, "I will take you back to Chalandri."

Lisa was drained and wordless on the trip back to Lazarus' farm. Every ounce of spirit seemed gone from her now—as though she had nothing left to fight what was torturing her mind.

Mike's head was dizzy with questions now. The choice of bolting again to the hills? The odds of trying to make his own contact for an escape boat? Each seemed futile. Whatever it was, Mike thought, she alone could solve it and he made his decision to remain.

They entered the pump house.

Lisa sat on the cot, drawn and weary.

"I am sorry," she said.

"Here, have some wine."

"Thank you."

She sipped the wine and a little color returned to her cheeks. She got up to leave. Mike looked at his watch.

"It is past curfew," he said.

She was silent.

"Go on," he said, "stretch out. . . . I'll—uh cover you with my jacket. Gets nippy during the night."

She took off her trench coat. Mike watched her delicate fingers loosen the bobby pins from her beret. He remembered how he used to love to watch Ellie undress. Lisa sat on the edge of the cot and kicked off her shoes. There was an awkward period.

"Seems—seems like we're always on cots," he mumbled. "Well, go on, stretch out. . . . I'll cover you up."

He pulled the heavy blanket from his cot and placed it over her gently as she curled up.

He knelt beside the cot and gazed at her. "I wish I could help you, Lisa," he said.

She took his hand and touched it to her lips. . . . "You are very sweet."

Mike's hand touched her golden hair and slid to her

cheek. Her eyes closed and again she looked like a small child. He kissed her forehead and she smiled.

Mike walked to the lamp and plunged the shack into darkness.

He lay restlessly on his cot and stared into the darkness. As he listened to the sound of her breathing, he remembered his sensations when he walked beside her, when he held her . . .

"Vassili," her voice called softly, "are you asleep?"

"No."

He heard her move in the darkness. . . .

The cot swayed. She was beside him. Her hand stroked his hair. "I will not let any harm come to you," she said.

He pulled her down beside him and found her lips. "Lisa—Lisa . . ."

Her hand pushed at his chest. "No, darling, no—don't be angry—please—don't be angry."

"It's—it's all right. You—you'd better get some sleep."

EIGHT

Two days passed. Lisa did not come. Mike was frantic.

He blamed the confinement, he blamed her beauty, he blamed the mystery and romance. All reason told him he was being foolish. Lisa was a woman he did not know, would never see again. Lisa might well be his enemy.

Rationalization failed. He had quite simply fallen in love with her.

He knew it was no novelty for men to fall in love with her. Perhaps she liked him and didn't wish to hurt his feelings.

Then he began to wonder about other things. . . . How many men had she been to bed with? What would it be like to love Lisa?

How strange—how very strange for this to happen! Mike knew that when Ellie died that love had died with him. There would never be the thrill of another romance . . . there would never be a love like Ellie.

Mike paced the dirt floor of the shack in Chalandri. . . . Was he destroying the memory of Ellie? Could he stifle this feeling for Lisa?

He remembered his first novel—a book about a man's one great love. His editor, in the cynical manner of most editors, argued that the "one great love" was a condition that existed only in fiction. In reality a man could have many loves in many times and each one of them true in its own way. His editor further argued that only in a book is a man willing to live forever with a memory. Mike knew now that his editor was right.

The contrast in loves and times was unexplainable. Ellie had been tall and fresh and bubbling and earthy. She had gone barefoot and had worn slacks and her happiest moments found her with a tennis racket in her hands or hiking through a backwoods trail or wrestling with Mike on a beach.

Lisa was frail, sad, queenly, shrouded in mystery.

Lisa knew—of that, Mike was certain. Only his declaration was missing. But he would never make it. He would chalk it up as a strange happening among many strange happenings and he'd forget her—sooner or later.

On the third day around noon he heard her footsteps coming up the path. She had never come this time of day before.

The door opened and Lisa entered. She seemed more lovely, more beautiful than he remembered her. She looked directly at him and spoke in a cold monotone.

"Tonight you will go into Athens alone. At nine o'clock take a sidewalk table at the Café Andreas on Constitution Square. A man named Nico will meet you. He will be wearing a black suit and have on a Mason's ring. Nico will take you to Dr. Thackery."

She turned around and opened the door.

"Lisa, will I see you again?"

"No," she answered and walked from the pump house.

NINE

Eight o'clock.

Mike put the pistol in his belt, took a last look around the pump house and stepped from the door.

The half-empty tram rolled toward Athens.

Eight-thirty.

Mike's stomach churned. At the intersection of Leophoros Alexandrou and Leophoros Kifissias he transferred to another tram—this one crowded. Many German soldiers were about. He shrank against the window and looked out. The tram rolled past the iron gate of the American Embassy. Two Marines in dress blues stood guard before it. Mike choked up at the sight of the American flag. The tram passed the Embassy.

The big clock over the square read ten minutes to nine. Mike crossed the street as he heard German heels click and guttural sputterings and flashy Italians passing by.

He looked into the cold eyes of a German officer. Mike reached to the ground and picked up the German's hat and bowed and apologized for bumping him in the crowd.

"Greek swine!"

"Efharisto!" Mike said and bowed again and edged away.

Café Andreas.

The sidewalk tables were nearly filled. Germans and their girls mostly. The sound of music reached Mike's ears. At a nearby table three Americans chatted.

There were hardly any Greek men about. Mike felt conspicuous and half-naked as he edged into a table near the curb. A waiter looked at him unhappily. Greeks were not welcome, Mike thought. He ordered a bottle of *krasi* and sat rigid, afraid to look to the right or the left. He took a long swig of wine, trying to relax.

Nine o'clock.

A streetwalker slinked past Mike's table and gave him the once over. She walked on in search of a more likely prospect. He poured another glass of *krasi* and drank it quickly.

Five past nine.

Ten past nine.

He was getting jumpy. Another glass of wine. The wine started to take hold. Mike looked over at the big clock. He'd give Nico just five minutes more to show up, then he'd leave.

"May I sit down?"

A hog-fat man was already pushing his way into a chair opposite Mike. He wore a ridiculous-looking panama squarely on the top of his head; his over-sized face looked like an English mastiff's. In one hand he balanced a dish of black olives and in the other, a drink. He popped an olive into his tiny mouth which was a slit between layers of hanging jowls. His eyes, too, were slits and seemed to stay open only with the greatest effort above two deep pouches. His suit was of a wrinkled white summer cloth.

"I am expecting someone," Mike said in Greek.

"Nico will not be here. He was—er—delayed."

The man spoke like an American. He lit a cigarette which seemed to get lost in his gargantuan face. He puffed slowly, eyeing Mike. Mike arose to move.

"I wouldn't go, if I were you. One outcry from me and you'd never get off the sidewalk."

Mike gulped down a glass of *krasi* in two swallows. The man cracked his knuckles and spoke again in an asthmatic wheeze. "You are a British escapee, is that not correct?"

Mike remained silent.

"You are, no doubt, in the market for a fast-moving boat for Egypt. Perhaps I could be of some assistance."

"I am a Greek citizen. I do not know what you are talking about."

"My dear fellow, I've been a correspondent in this country for twelve years. I know a Greek when I see one."

"All right—so I'm British."

"Now then, that's better."

The man lifted his fingers and beckoned the waiter

for another bottle of *krasi*. Mike looked around for a
means of escape. There was none. The place swarmed
with Germans.

"Now then," he said, "I take it you would like to
take leave of this pleasant little country."

"What's your game?" Mike snapped.

"Game? My dear fellow, I am Julius Chesney, foreign correspondent for the New York *Star Bulletin*.
Have you ever read my reports? They are very illumi-
nating. They are carried in the London *Times*."

"I'm a New Zealander."

"Good. I like New Zealanders, stout fellows." He
smacked his lips on another olive and dug his fingers
into his mouth to locate the pit. The *krasi* arrived. "Just
say it is a little avocation of mine. I take pleasure in
helping you boys."

"I'm listening. I have no choice."

"Suppose I told you I was in contact with the captain
of an unusually fast boat who knew the mine fields and
the patrol schedules and the way to North Africa."

"Suppose you did."

"How much value would you place on it?"

"I have no idea."

"Is it worth—er—say three million to hit a nice
round figure?"

"I don't have that kind of money."

"Small matter. It just so happens I also know of a
lovely Greek family who would be most happy to
underwrite your passage."

"Look, Chesney. I've heard about your little racket.
You produce me to some Greek family, collect your
money for my passage and the boat never shows up.
Then you collect another fat reward for turning me
over to the Gestapo."

"My *dear* fellow," Chesney held up his fat hand in

protest. "By all appearances you've had some dealings with—er—unsavory characters."

"You don't look like the keeper of the privy seal to me."

He contorted his fleshy face into what may have been mistaken for a smile. "I like you. . . . What is your name?"

"Smith—Joe Smith."

"Come, come."

"Linden—Jay Linden."

The conversation stopped as a German and his girl hovered nearby searching for an empty table. They drifted away.

Mike leaned over the table. "Look, Mr. Chesney, I wouldn't trust you any further than I could throw a bull by the horns. Now be a good fellow and let me go."

"Sit still, Linden, sit still," he wheezed. Chesney sipped his drink and drummed his fat fingers on the table slowly. Mike gritted his teeth in discomfort. "Let me put my cards on the table. Perhaps if I presented my proposition in a more—er—open light, you'd like to . . ."

"All right—shoot."

"You came here to contact Nico. Nico or the Underground can't help you. Heilser and his Greek friend, Zervos, know every move they are making. You have heard of Herr Heilser, haven't you?"

"I've heard his name mentioned."

Mike had to admit to himself that Chesney was certainly well informed.

"Man to man, plain and simple. My hobby is collecting drachmas. I like drachmas—you represent a lot of them to me."

"Why don't you open up a whorehouse?"

Chesney smiled. "To repeat an old cliché—too many amateurs are ruining the business these days. Escapees are much more profitable." He wheezed and placed his hand to his chest. "I'm getting along in years—bad heart. Let us say I'm starting a little nest egg."

"Dealing in hot British skins."

"My dear fellow. Escapees are all the rage these days. In some quarters I'm looked upon as quite a martyr."

"How do I know you won't doublecross me?" Mike said.

"You don't know, except for my honest face."

Mike was forced to smile. Moreover, Chesney interested him. He was obviously a slick operator—well informed and there was a fifty-fifty chance he was on the level. It would do no harm to string him out, Mike thought.

"What's your deal?"

"Good. I see you are a man of sound judgment, Linden. Now meet me at the Piccadilly Café off Concord Square this Thursday at noon. Mr. Choleva, your benefactor, will want to meet you. He has already sponsored four escapees. All of them are safe in Egypt, I may add."

"Do you know what's going to happen if you cross me, Chesney?"

"No—tell me."

"I'll kill you."

Chesney sighed. "My dear fellow. That was quite hammy and entirely uncalled for. Now, see those two gentlemen across the street?"

Mike looked over Chesney's shoulder. A pair of civilians in German-cut clothes leaned against a building feigning conversation with each other.

"Those two chaps are Gestapo. They hang about the Square just hoping British boys like you will drop in. It appears that you've been spotted. Now, Mr. Linden, if your brain is as large as your mouth you should have no trouble in shaking them. They are quite stupid. I'll see you on Thursday, Piccadilly Café."

Mike's heart skipped a beat as Julius Chesney arose and waddled away.

TEN

Mike gulped down another half glass of *krasi*. The two Gestapo men across the street watched. He got to his feet, rubber-legged, and started to cross the square. The two men began to follow some distance behind him. Mike quickened his pace and fought off an impulse to break into a run.

He turned the corner and passed a row of shops. Halfway down the block, he paused, looked into a window on which there was a sign, Anton's Dress Shop, and lit a cigarette.

The two Gestapo men sped around the corner and stopped abruptly when they saw Mike.

Mike looked about frantically. A tram was coming to a stop at the intersection down the block. He quickly crossed the street. The tram moved past the intersection, picked up speed and bore down toward the middle of the block where Mike stood. It came closer—closer—closer. . . .

Mike leaped from the curb onto the tram, almost

tearing his arm from its socket. He stumbled onto the rear platform as the tram rolled full speed past the pursuers.

Mike looked down the street. He saw an automobile roll to a stop beside the two Gestapo men. One of them pointed to the tram and the car began to follow a block behind him.

The tram slowed for a stop. Mike jumped off and sprinted into a dark street.

Where? Where? Where?

He was limp with fright. In the middle of the block he came to an alleyway. He could hear the car turn the corner down the block.

Mike plunged into the pitch-black alley and ran the length of it—only to hit a dead end. A fifteen-foot brick wall sealed his exit. He leaped up, but his hand fell short of the top. On the other side of the wall came the sound of barking dogs.

Mike squinted desperately into the darkness. The backs of houses faced him on both sides. A few yellow lights glinted through drawn shades. The putrid smell of garbage reached his nostrils. ... A rat darted past him over the slimy cobblestones.

He flattened against the wall and drew his pistol.

At the far end of the alley he heard car doors slam, then footsteps and half-whispered orders.

Mike slunk along the wall and along some low fences past several houses. The beam of a flashlight darted into the alley. He tumbled over a fence and crouched behind it. At the end of the alley he heard another car screech to a stop.

"Is someone out there?" a voice called behind Mike.

He spun around. The back door to a house was opened.

"Englezos," he croaked ... "Englezos—help me ..."

"In here, quickly," the voice answered.

The door shut behind him. Mike fell against it panting and dizzy. A woman stood before him clad only in a kimono. "Follow me," she said.

They turned into a long hallway. She snapped a door open. Mike reeled into the room. "Stay here," the woman said. "I will return in a few minutes."

He collapsed into a chair and buried his head in his hands. "Jesus ... Jesus Christ ..."

He lifted his head and looked around the room slowly. It was lit by a blue bulb in a lamp behind a satin-covered bed. A gaudy chaise longue was near the bed. On one wall, the usual ikon and picture of Christ. In sharp contrast, on the other walls, hung several reproductions of Greek paintings. All of them depicted naked young ladies in various stages of repose. There was an alcove beside the bed. It was partly concealed by a heavy curtain but Mike could see a sink and basin stand.

He stiffened at the sound of laughter and talk in the hallway. One voice was that of a German, the other a Greek woman's.

Several times, doors opened and closed nearby.

Then quiet.

There was a soft tap on his door and it was opened. The woman in the kimono stepped in quickly and bolted it behind her. "Gestapo are all over the street," she said. "They are throwing a ring around the entire neighborhood."

Mike stood up and wiped the sweat from his face.

"You can put your pistol away. You will be safe here."

He watched her walk to the chaise longue and stretch

out on it. She was young, in her mid-twenties, and not without some beauty. She smiled at Mike. "My name is Ketty," she said. "Be a dear and rub the back of my neck."

He stumbled over to her. She slipped the kimono from her shoulders, baring half her bosom. Mike stood awkwardly behind her. "Don't be bashful," Ketty said.

She purred as his hands massaged her neck and shoulders. "That feels wonderful. We all wish so badly the Englezos were back. You were all such gentlemen. These Germans are louts. And the Macaronades! Each one thinks he is the greatest lover in the world. I've been working since noon," she rambled on. . . . "They argue even about the little they pay. It doesn't matter much, drachmas are dropping in value every day."

Ketty put her kimono back on and touched her hair. "Don't be frightened—half the German Command is here."

"You're very sweet, Ketty. I won't forget this."

"It is nice talking to an Englezos again. It was good the short time they were here. I have a little girl, you know."

"Is that right?"

"Yes. She is a very lovely child. She stays at the convent. It is quite expensive but she is a rare child— quite gifted. I'm so proud. I hope I am able to keep her there. With money meaning so little these days—I just don't know."

Mike peeled off a million drachmas from his roll.

"Oh, no!" Ketty protested. "I did not mean that. I would not take money from you."

"For your daughter."

"No—no—you will need it. You will need it for a boat to Africa."

"Don't argue." He put the money on the dresser.

"You are very nice. What is your name?"

"Jay."

"That is what I like about the Englezos. Their names are so simple."

Their conversation stopped as a German argued with a girl outside the door.

"Dogs—dogs—always arguing. There is some wine in the night stand. Pour yourself a glass."

"I've had enough to drink."

She walked over to him and smiled. "You are a nice man, Jay. Would you like to go to bed with me?"

"I'm just not in the mood right now, honey. . . ."

"I understand. . . ."

A staccato knock on the door. Ketty opened it a crack and held a whispered conversation with the woman on the other side. She turned to Mike. "Soldiers outside with Gestapo. They are going to search. Get into the alcove and draw the curtain. Don't move a muscle."

Mike obeyed.

In another moment he heard the door open. He heard Ketty greet a man in an amorous voice. The man laughed and Ketty squealed in pretended delight as they moved about the room. The man spoke in German. He heard the smack of a kiss.

He heard the German grunting as he pulled off his boots.

The bed creaked just a few feet from where Mike stood flat against a wall. Amorous moans—kisses—the bed creaking faster . . .

A smashing rap on the door. "Gestapo!" a voice boomed.

Mike heard the German stumble into his trousers, sputtering oaths. The door opened.

"What the hell is this!"

"Major! Forgive us, but a British escapee is in the area."

"Well, he isn't in here, dammit!"

The door slammed.

The hours passed. It was two A.M.

Ketty came to the room once more and flopped to the bed, exhausted. "Those louts never go home," she mumbled. "There are three drunks in the parlor now. . . . There are some of them that like to beat the girls. . . ."

She rose and drew the curtain to the alcove and splashed cold water on her face.

As Mike began to get his bearings, he planned his next move. Obviously Lisa could not be trusted and he boiled over at the thought that she had duped him.

There was hilly country and a forest near Chalandri. He would hide out there. It was three days till Thursday and he would keep the appointment with Julius Chesney at the Piccadilly Café.

He told himself it was foolish to return to Chalandri, but he seethed with anger at himself as he realized he would try to see Lisa again.

"I'll leave just as soon as it turns light," Mike said.

Ketty was wiping her face with a towel. "Do you have a place to stay?"

"Yes, in Chalandri."

"I'd better drive you out there now, before it turns light."

"What about the curfew?"

Ketty smiled sarcastically. "There are some things the Germans do not put a curfew on. I am allowed to travel. You are welcome to stay here, if you like."

"It's out of the question."

"I'll give you my phone number. You can never tell when you'll need me."

ELEVEN

Four A.M.

The night was star-studded. Mike skirted the lemon grove on Lazarus' farm. The ground began to rise at the boundary of the field. He came to a ditch.

It would be dangerous to continue without more light. A stray dog could upset everything if he crossed a strange field. The forest was several kilometers away— a good hour's hike.

Mike scooted down into the ditch and decided to wait out the night. From the rise he could see the full stretch of the farm and the farmhouse and the outlines of the pump house.

He was still shaken from the events of the night, but he was so bleary-eyed and exhausted that he dozed off. It was close to freezing in the ditch.

Mike rolled over and blew into his hands and flexed his fingers and massaged his numbed legs. A gray tint of dawn and a rooster crowing at a nearby farm. He stumbled from the ditch and looked around. Now he could see the murky outline of the hills and the distant forest. He would chance it now.

As he glanced across the farm he heard a strange

sound coming from the lemon grove. He saw a shadowy figure flitting among the trees. Then—a crack of light from the pump house.

Mike stood frozen . . . Ten minutes—fifteen . . .

A look of rage came into his face. His hand was on his pistol. He walked slowly down the rise toward the pump house.

His foot kicked against the door and it flew open.

"Vassili! Thank God!"

"Don't thank God me, you bitch!"

Lisa fell against him sobbing. He shoved her away and she fell on a cot. He closed the door.

"You fool! You wretched fool!" she sobbed. "Nico was picked up by the Gestapo. He is in Averof Prison . . . Dr. Thackery is in hiding. . . ."

She stopped, arose and came close to Mike. He leveled the pistol at her. She raised her hand and smacked his cheek. Mike smacked her back.

They glared at each other in hatred. . . .

"The Gestapo may know of this place now," she said. "We have another place for you."

Mike remained motionless, his pale-blue eyes piercing her.

She stepped around him and walked to the door.

He spun around, seized her arm and pulled her close to him.

"What are you up to now?" he said, shaking her violently.

"Vassili! Vassili! I almost lost my mind!"

"Oh, Lisa . . . Lisa . . ."

Her fingers tore at his hair and she pulled his face to her lips. . . .

"Lisa . . . Lisa . . . Lisa . . ."

"No, darling . . . No—we can't—we can't . . . It's not safe here . . . The Gestapo may come. . . ."

He scooped her into his arms and walked toward the cot. "To hell with the Gestapo. . . ."

Mike knelt beside the cot and traced the lines of her satiny body. She smiled and kissed him.

Lisa was at peace for the first time since she had known him. As for Mike, she had fulfilled his every dream and answered every unanswered question.

But it was Mike, not Lisa who showed remorse. He knew he had sentenced himself to another term of haunting loneliness. He had fallen desperately, hopelessly in love. It was all too unreal, a fantasy . . .

"Vassili," she whispered, "this is shameless. It would be terribly embarrassing if the Gestapo were to pay us a visit."

"Yes, I suppose we'd better leave."

He helped her to her feet and their bodies pressed together.

"Are you sorry?"

"Of course not, Vassili. I love you."

Mike and Lisa entered a brick mansion at Satovriandou, 125, in Athens. The place was empty, unfurnished and felt haunted. He followed her up three flights of a circular stairway guarded by a massive mahogany rail. The house echoed its emptiness.

On the third floor they walked down a dusty hall to a door. Lisa unlocked the door which led to another flight of stairs. The steps creaked under their weight.

She ushered him into a meagerly furnished garret.

"I must leave now."

They embraced and kissed.

"I'll hurry back as soon as I can," she whispered.

TWELVE

His last cigarette was gone. He lay on the bed beside the slanting garret window and looked out at the hills of Athens. It was turning dark and lights began to come on.

In a way it reminded him of San Francisco.

It was very quiet in the garret. He remembered another time—the day he was in the hills looking down at Kalámai. Athens was stricken and suffering but now she looked peaceful, as though she was ready to fall into an untroubled slumber.

He closed his eyes and waited for Lisa's return. He thought about the morning in the pump house. He was tense with wanting her . . .

Night.

An echo thundered through the empty house. He opened his eyes and saw the aura of lights around the city. He heard Lisa's footsteps moving up the long circular stair. His blood boiled as they neared. The door clicked open and he felt her presence in the dark room.

"Vassili?" her half-frightened voice called.

"Here—by the window."

A bluish light filtered over the room. Her shadow preceded her toward him. She stood over the bed and their hands touched.

He watched as she raised her arms and whisked off

her dress, and his breath deepened unevenly as she stood silent and naked before him.

She bent over him and her hands touched his body softly and her lips brushed his. He reached up and drew her down and he felt the wonder of her body against his. They united, gently, quietly . . .

He studied her body as she rolled against him with a sleepy, contented sigh. He reached up and turned off the light over the bed and they lay in each other's arms and looked out at the city.

"I'll come back for you some day," he said.

She shook her head slowly. "I love you, Vassili. Let us be grateful for these few hours and not think of something a century from now."

"It's so fantastic that this should happen."

"It is not fantastic. I think I loved you the moment I saw you in the cottage in Kaloghriani. I did not think I was capable of feeling this way again about anyone."

"That's funny," he said. "I guess we're two of a kind."

Lisa left his side abruptly and sat on the edge of the bed with her back to him. "A British submarine is coming for you tomorrow night."

Deathly silence.

The first traces of a new day showed on the hills of Athens. He took her arm and drew her down beside him. "Don't get dressed yet."

"All right, darling."

"I wish I were very eloquent and could tell you . . ."

"Shhh—shhh . . . You are like a little boy when you try to speak. . . ."

They sat in front of the garret window having dinner at daybreak. Steaks and wine. Mike loaded his pipe with the last pinch of tobacco he had.

"You know, Vassili, the Germans could soften up the rear ends of their cows a bit."

"No excuses because you're a bad cook."

A feathery cloud formed outside their window and the hills faded from sight.

"This is a good day for . . ." but Mike cut it short.

"A good day for what, dear?"

"Nothing."

He was about to say, "A good day for writing." Somehow he could always write better when the weather was nasty. Just a writer's quirk, he thought.

She cleared the dishes and they lingered over cups of ersatz coffee. He gazed at the softness which was revealed through her unbuttoned dress front.

He was blind with love for her. Lisa was an enchanted dream and he had wandered into her enchantment.

"Lisa, tell me about yourself. . . ."

"It is not very pleasant. . . ."

"Please . . ."

All her sadness seemed to return. She looked away from him and through the misted window and her mind drifted into a haunted past. . . .

It had been a good life. Her mother, an Englishwoman of great beauty. Her father, a gentle little man who owned a small prosperous factory. Lisa and her sister had finished their studies at the university and, encouraged by her father's love of music, she had studied piano at the conservatories in Rome and Paris. Her sister had become a doctor of literature.

A close family . . . A concert career coming . . . Just about all the fulfillment one could ask of life. Then, a foolish, heady, whirlwind romance with an ambitious young engineer which ended in marriage. Lisa learned the extent of his ambition after the German occupation. He absconded with the family money, the factory and her two sons.

Her mother, fortunately, did not live to see this happen. Lisa had not believed her gentle father to be a man of great courage, but he showed it at his death in Averof Prison.

"And your sister?"

"She lives with a German officer."

There was more to Lisa's story, Mike felt, but he asked no more.

She buttoned her dress and put on her trench coat and beret in front of a small stained mirror.

"There are many arrangements to be made. I will return as early as possible."

She stopped at the door and turned to him.

"I suppose it was foolish of us to have fallen in love."

Mike paced the room like a crazy man. It would take all the courage he had to leave her now. He was obsessed with love for her.

Maybe the Underground would let her leave Greece. . . .

Maybe he'd turn the Stergiou list over to them and stay on. . . .

Maybe he'd escape to the hills with her and hide out. . . .

The day became a hell of confusion. How far would he go to keep her?

The wall of doubt closed in tighter.

If only he could accept their few hours of happiness in the same way she had accepted them.

The only thing that was real to Mike was the heartless ticking of the clock and the thought that it would all be over soon.

He knew he would have to pay for this love somehow. He became calm. There was no other way. Somehow, he would find the courage to leave her.

Lisa's face was pale and filled with worry. "Something has gone wrong, Vassili. The submarine will not be here."

They clung to each other.

"Dear God! What are we going to do?" she cried.

Lisa pressed herself against Mike. He was exhausted but sleepless. He was dangerously close to the breaking point. Her continued presence sapped the will from him. He drew the blanket over them and turned to look out of the rain-spattered window.

He knew now what he would have to do. Another day—two—three of lingering farewells—impossible . . . He would keep his appointment with Julius Chesney tomorrow.

Thursday.

Mike had hoped Lisa would be gone. It would have been easier.

The clock read ten past eleven.

He put on his jacket and tucked the pistol into his belt.

"What are you doing, Vassili?"

"I'm going out."

"Have you lost your mind?"

Mike walked toward the door. She blocked his passage.

"Vassili! What is the matter with you?"

"I said I'm going out."

"Are you insane? The Gestapo will have you within an hour."

"I can't take it any more, Lisa . . ."

"Darling," she cried, "our people are working day and night! Another few days . . ."

"Can't you see what's happened? Do you want me to disgrace myself? Do you want me to crawl?"

She fell against him. Her fingers worked nervously, grasping and releasing his arms. "It is my fault for wanting you. I'll go away, if that's what you want."

"It will be just as bad that way."

He whirled her around and bolted through the door.

"Vassili!"

He stopped for an instant at the front door and looked up.

She stood at the top of the circular stairs, her fingers tearing frantically at her clothes. "Vassili! No! No!"

He closed the door behind him.

THIRTEEN

Concord Square.

Mike stood across the street from the Piccadilly Café. There seemed little activity about. He wondered if he was making a mistake. But it seemed that Lisa was making him do foolish things. He hedged and began to turn back.

"Ah, Jay Linden, right on time. I see you got rid of your two traveling companions."

Mike wheeled around and looked into the mastiff face of Julius Chesney. A second man, apparently a seaman, stood alongside him.

"Well, let us not stand here on the sidewalk, dear fellow. I believe a noonday nip is in order," Chesney wheezed. "Come along. I didn't bring the German army with me. My friend here is Antonis, the captain of the *Arkadia*."

The three entered the café and found an isolated booth. They ordered *krasi*. Mike studied Antonis, who seemed oblivious as he puffed away on his pipe.

Chesney, talking in whispers, told Mike the *Arkadia* was a small, trim and fast motorboat that carried a crew of three. The ship's papers would read: Crete, but actual destination would be Cairo. Antonis, Mike was assured, knew the route well, having made two other trips with British escapees. Mike's sponsor, the man who was going to pay for his passage, was due to join them shortly.

"When do we sail?" Mike asked.

"As soon as we get another escapee to man the boat."

"Since I saw you last I raised some money. If Antonis and I can handle the boat between us, I'll buy the passage."

The leathery old sailor nodded. He reckoned he and Mike could handle the ship.

"Four million drachmas," Chesney shot out quickly.

"Aren't you stretching it?"

"You are the one who seems eager to leave."

"I'll give you three million if we sail tonight."

Chesney scratched his jowls. "Let me see your money."

Mike placed his bundle of cash on the table. For the first time, Julius Chesney showed emotion. His fat jowls quivered. His fleshy hand darted over the table. Mike grabbed his wrist.

"You take half now—half when we get underway."

Chesney looked at the money, sighed and withdrew his hand and watched Mike carefully as he counted off a million and a half drachmas. Chesney re-counted the money, his eyes watering.

A small, gray-haired man entered the café and looked around.

"Ah, here comes another three million drachmas," Chesney said. "Over here, Mr. Cholevas!" he called.

The well-dressed elderly gentleman slipped quietly into the booth and nodded to everyone.

"Jay, meet your sponsor. The benevolent friend of the British, Mr. Apostolos Cholevas."

Cholevas nodded quietly.

Mike was curious about the man. He wondered why he was doing this.

"What good is my money if the Germans take over my country?" Mr. Cholevas stayed long enough to have a half glass of wine and to give the money to Chesney. He wished Mike a good trip and asked if perhaps he'd write after the war. The old gentleman departed with a last request—to be sure to let the British know what was happening in Greece.

Julius Chesney cracked his knuckles, chewed a biscuit and then drew a sheaf of papers from his crumpled suit. He spread them out on the table.

Arkadia: Destination: Crete.

"Do you have identification papers, Linden?"

Mike produced the card and papers that bore the name, Vassili Papadopoulos. "Good—good—this saves me an expense." Chesney wrote the name on the ship's papers.

"Now, I believe everything is in order. The gas will be aboard before dark, gentlemen. Antonis, meet me later and I'll have the clearance papers and the patrol schedules."

"What about inspection of the boat?" Mike asked.

"My *dear* fellow. Do you cast aspersions on my ability? Ah me, by the time I finish oiling everyone's palm there is so little left. So many fingers in the pot, and prices are just outrageous these days. Well, Linden, do have a pleasant journey and do read my column when you get to London."

Chesney shoved his way out of the booth and patted the pocket filled with drachmas affectionately. He extended his hand.

"Do be careful, Michael Morrison," Chesney said. "It would be extremely regrettable if the Stergiou list were to fall into German hands."

Mike stood there, dumbstruck, as Julius Chesney waddled from the café.

Part 4

ONE

Lisa sat at the far end of the table and looked over at the four pairs of grim eyes fixed on her. The candle on the center of the table cast a dancing shadow on the bare walls of the room.

Three of the men she had known since childhood. Only the strange, stony Dr. Harry Thackery was new to her.

"It was impossible to stop him," she cried.

Papa-Panos, the priest, his beard now gray ... Huge, moon-faced Michalis, the union organizer, who always wore the scowl of an angry lion ... Gentle, scholarly Thanassis, the professor at the university ...

There was silence as Lisa shook her head and gripped the edge of the table.

Michalis' hamlike fist pounded on the table and the candle bounced. "Why didn't you follow him?" he roared.

Lisa did not answer.

"Lisa," Dr. Thackery said, "you were under orders to kill him in the event something like this happened.

Do you realize the consequences if he falls into German hands?"

Her mouth was dry. She closed her eyes and licked her parched lips. "I did not know who he was," she whispered.

"I ask you again, Lisa, why didn't you follow him?" Michalis repeated.

"Well, Lisa?" Dr. Thackery added.

She sighed and lowered her head. "I was not dressed."

"Undressed!"

"For goodness' sake, Michalis, quiet down," the soft-spoken Thanassis said. "As usual, your voice can be heard in Salonika."

"I do not hide that I love him!" Lisa cried.

Papa-Panos, the priest, had sat listening quietly. He stroked the end of his beard. At last he spoke in his high-pitched voice that never failed to carry authority. "Thanassis—Michalis—Dr. Thackery—I seriously wonder if all of us are not wrong about this Morrison. Would it not be wise that we all just forget about him?"

"Are you insane, Father?"

"Do not raise your voice to me, Michalis. You are not speaking in a union hall. Suppose Morrison does escape . . . Suppose he does turn the names over to the British . . . Have any of you thought what would happen then? It means we will be compelled to act on their information. And, gentlemen, we cannot expect the Germans to sit by idly. They will retaliate in triple measure—of that you can be certain. We can look forward to the slaughter of hundreds of innocents."

"Bah," Michalis grumbled. He leaned over the table and pointed his finger almost into Papa-Panos' beard. "Are we receiving milk and honey from the Germans now? Only yesterday the Nazi butchers massacred a hundred civilians in Crete. If our people do not have guns they will fight back with rocks and sticks. Is it better to die with a gun in your hand or a pitchfork?"

"It is one thing to aid British escapees or to seek food. It is another to signal a mass uprising," Papa-Panos said. "When the British begin smuggling in arms, they will be used—and who here thinks we can defeat the German army?"

Thanassis interrupted. "As much as I love and respect you, Father, I must agree with Michalis. Passive resistance has proved fruitless. The cities and the hills are angry and our people will fight."

"And do you agree with them, Dr. Thackery?"

The bony-faced man remained silent for many moments. "I do not choose sides," he finally said. "It is not my affair. We know that the British will establish a mission here when they receive the Stergiou list. It means that we must organize and act on information about arms shipments, train schedules, troop movements, submarines . . . It means the British will ship in arms to help us carry out missions. We know, too, that the Germans will destroy villages and cities and kill your citizens for every act we commit against them. What is our gain? If we become strong—if we can place enough pressure on the Germans, they will be forced to keep their troops here and will not be able to release them for fighting on the main fronts. Neither you nor I can stop the Greek people from striking back. Truly, Papa-Panos, the hills are angry."

The priest sighed. He knew these men spoke the truth. Greece was destined for a blood bath that would make all the ancient tragedies trivial by comparison. He nodded his head slowly. "Very well, we will spare no expense in finding the American and getting him out of the country."

Then the four of them turned to Lisa. Her lips were white. She arose slowly and spoke. "Before you make a decision, there is more I must tell you now."

In slow, deliberate words, Lisa unfolded her story beginning with the day that the Gestapo had picked her up and taken her to Conrad Heilser. The four men looked shocked. Then she told of the weeks of terror and ended her story at the point where Morrison had dashed from the apartment at Satovriandou, 125.

She asked no mercy. The men sat in horrified silence. Lisa walked straight and proud to the door. "I shall wait in the next room," she said.

She felt as though life itself was gone now. What did it matter? She had lost her children and she had lost him. At least she had purged herself. . . .

Through the paper-thin walls she heard Michalis pound his fist on the table.

"Lisa Kyriakides is a traitor to the Greek people!"

Thanassis shook his head in disbelief. His studious appearance belied the fact that he was one of the most daring men in the movement. "Lisa—I can't believe it—I can't believe it. I have known her since she was a girl of sixteen. She was a student of mine at the university. I brought her in to our organization. . . ."

"I too have known her and her family for many years," Michalis said. "We cannot let sentimentality rule us." He spoke as one who had lived a life of iron-clad discipline. He felt no sympathy for those who failed to perform their duty. He had dealt too long with too many of those who played both sides.

"It seems we have no choice," Thanassis said. "But I will not be the man to pull the trigger."

Thackery said nothing. This was not his matter.

"If she was a traitor, would she have told us her story?" Papa-Panos said.

"Do not be taken in by female tricks, Father. She is a marked woman. She came to us first in hopes we would be more merciful than the Germans. If we are to maintain discipline in this organization we have no choice."

"And by her execution we place ourselves on the same level with the Nazis. . . ."

"And what do you propose we do? Pray, perhaps, to get her to repent?"

"Quiet! I have heard enough of your ranting for one day, Michalis. Lisa is no more a traitor than I am. Do we not already have enough killing? Remember, she is the daughter of Ioannis Rodites, a martyr of the Greek people. Is your memory so short you cannot remember the first man in Athens to recognize your union without bloodshed?"

"Do not dishonor the name of Ioannis Rodites," Michalis shot back. "What of her sister, Maria Rodites, a whore for a German officer? What of her husband, Manolis Kyriakides, a filthy collaborator?" He spat on the floor.

"Hasn't this woman had enough sorrow to bear? Surely, Michalis, you must realize that if she had treason in her heart she could have become the mistress of Konrad Heilser. She could have the wealth of Athens at her feet. You seem to forget she only did this to protect the lives of her two sons."

"I am the father of a son also," Michalis said. "I speak to you as a man who loves him as I love life itself. I would rather see him in his grave than see his father become a collaborator."

"Yes, Michalis," Papa-Panos answered. "Perhaps you would see your son in his grave. But tell me something, would your wife?"

TWO

The *Arkadia* was neither fast nor trim. She was an out-sized mud scow and Mike wondered if she was seaworthy.

"Go below," Antonis said in his longest speech of the day.

The cabin held four bunks, a galley and a head. Mike stretched out and could see up the ladder topside where Antonis stood by the rail, puffing away on his pipe and looking alternately from water to sky.

Although riddled with anxiety, Mike began to feel a certain security. So far, Julius Chesney had delivered. One thought comforted him. Somehow, Chesney knew his true identity and he knew of the Stergiou list. Perhaps Chesney was overdramatizing his love of drachmas, for Mike knew that his capture by the Germans would have brought Chesney ten times the passage money. Mike also felt an instinctive trust in the silent skipper, Antonis. Mike began to relax.

After standing motionless for an hour at the rail, Antonis poked his head into the cabin, his pipe, as weatherbeaten as his face, firmly clenched in his teeth. "I go for the clearance papers."

It had all gone smoothly, Mike thought, almost too smoothly. At the dock gates of Piraeus there had not been so much as a raised eyebrow from the guards when Mike had passed through with Antonis. Mike credited Julius Chesney with knowing his business.

He did, however, underestimate the man's love of drachmas. In a half hour, Antonis returned to the boat with two men and a girl.

In the cabin, a bull of a man, an Australian named Ben Masterton, introduced himself. The other man was a sallow-faced lad of about twenty, a Palestinian named Yichiel. At Yichiel's side stood a frightened girl, his wife, Elpis, who said she was going to join the free Greek forces in Egypt.

Mike was going to protest to Antonis about the extra passage money. He had been bilked, but he decided to do nothing. He was thankful he'd have someone other than Antonis to talk to during the voyage. Then, the other three would serve as a good covering force— safety in numbers—and give the trip the air of being a routine escape.

The Greek police went through the motions of an inspection, stamped the clearance papers and the *Arkadia* chugged away from the dock. Chesney had apparently oiled their palms well. Mike became uneasy about the slickness of the operation. It just couldn't be this easy, he thought.

The sea air was chilly.

Young Yichiel and his bride went to the cabin and huddled close on a single bunk and began to whisper softly.

Mike envied him. How he envied him!

The hills of Athens grew smaller and smaller. Somewhere in Athens there was a garret apartment . . . Only last night, he and Lisa . . . Mike was sinking into a state of moroseness.

The *Arkadia* cleared the harbor area. Antonis stopped the engine and dropped anchor.

"What in 'ell's comin' off?" Ben Masterton demanded.

"We stay till dawn. German orders. British submarines. If we move, a patrol boat will stop us."

"Well, I don't like it."

"Do not tell me my business," Antonis said, ending the discussion.

They waited out the hours at anchor. Mike never took his eyes from the hills of Athens. He was overwhelmed with sadness.

Darkness fell.

Yichiel and Elpis slept locked in each other's arms in the cabin below. Antonis stood at the rail, looking from water to sky.

Ben Masterton sat aft on the deck near Mike, his back against the rail. He began to sing softly.

The Australian bull fancied himself a concert singer. He sang his way through all of the old numbers of the baritone repertoire with most of the time-worn hammed-up gestures of a baritone. His left hand caressed his beard and his right arm swept the air.

Mike liked Masterton. Earlier the Australian had told him of his four previous attempts to escape, only to get so drunk that he tried to whip the entire German Army.

"Hey, Linden," Masterton whispered, sliding close to Mike.

"Yes?"

"Look. I don't make it a habit of drinkin' with New Zealanders, but I likes the cut of you." Ben pulled a bottle from his jacket.

"Brandy—just what the doctor ordered."

"Shhhh, not so loud, you bloomin' fool. We'll be splittin' it five ways when there ain't rightly enough for the two of us."

Mike took a long swig and tried to burn the hurt out

of himself. Ben yanked the bottle from Mike's lips and drank, matching Mike's swig.

The level of the bottle moved downward quickly.

Ben scratched his head, looked at the empty bottle and flipped it over the rail. "You goddamn Kiwi," he said. "I shoulda knowd better'n to drink with a goddamn Kiwi. . . ."

"Aw, shaddup, 'less you wanna take a bath, Masterton. . . ."

"I likes the cut of you, Linden." Ben's powerful arm went around Mike's shoulders. "Tell you what . . . I likes you so much I'm gonna let you sing a duet wiff me—that's how much I likes you. Too bad you wasn't wiff me when I whipped fourteen of them spaghetti eaters—fourteen of 'em, see. . . . Mos' fun I ever had . . . what'll we sing, matey?"

"Don' feel like singing, Ben. . . . Don' feel like singing. There's a broad in Athens—goddamn broad in a goddamn 'partment and I want that broad . . ."

"Aw, come now, matey—don' cry—don' cry . . ."

"Can't hep it. . . . What that goddamn broad . . ."

"Le's sing London Dairy Air—les you got a version to a good English song . . ."

"Thatsa tenor song, you ignorant slob."

"Linden! I can sing anything—'cluding souprano."

Soft grunts came from the cabin. Ben got on all fours and began crawling toward it. Mike grabbed him by the belt and dragged him back. "Leave 'em alone, you bastard. . . ."

"Goddamit, Linden, thatsa last time I drink with a Kiwi—very last time. . . ."

They put their arms around each other's shoulders and blended in dubious harmony.

Antonis held his pose by the fore rail.

The noise in the cabin subsided.

The *Arkadia* heaved gently under a swell.

Suddenly Antonis took his foot from the rail and stood tense, as if listening. Mike poked Ben in the ribs and they both stared hard through their alcoholic haze.

The distant sound of a motor reached their ears.

Mike and Ben stumbled to their feet and went fore beside Antonis.

"Let's get this pisspot moving," Masterton said.

"Hold still," Antonis ordered. "They may turn away."

Mike felt his guts turn over. A minute passed, and the motor seemed to fade away. Suddenly it became louder and louder.

"I say let's get underway!" Masterton roared with the sweat pouring down his face.

The boat was coming close now. They could see its outline about four hundred yards to the starboard side.

Yichiel and Elpis scrambled topside, bug-eyed in terror. The girl buried her head in the boy's chest.

A siren shrieked.

A flash of light streaked across the water. It settled on the *Arkadia* and caught the five of them in its beam. The motor roared in louder.

"*Arkadia!*" a voice boomed in the darkness, "stand by to be boarded!"

THREE

A semi-circle of German soldiers at fixed bayonets waited on the dock as the patrol boat eased in. Mike was stupefied with fear. A wave of nausea swept through him as he set foot on the pier. He closed his eyes dizzily. Ben's strong hand gripped his shoulder. A caged truck drove up. The five were thrown in. A convoy of armed cars escorted the truck. Sirens cleared a path and the convoy sped from the docks onto the highway toward Athens.

Fool—fool—fool—fool! Madness to do business with Julius Chesney! Madness to fall in love!

Elpis sobbed in the arms of her sallow-faced Palestinian, Yichiel. But Antonis showed no anxiety. He puffed his pipe complacently and stared through the barred door at the rear of the truck.

Ben started to mumble to himself. "I got myself drunk last night. . . . I must have shot off my mouth. . . ."

The convoy arrived at the outskirts of Athens.

"Where will they take us?" Mike whispered hoarsely.

"Averof Prison," Ben said. "Get a hold on yourself, matey, they're all bluff. . . ."

The five captives were taken to a room with walls and floors of stone. Arrayed about them were two dozen brown-shirted Nazis armed with pistols and clubs.

Behind a desk sat Colonel Oberg, the Commandant of Averof Prison. He had a classic Prussian face, complete with monocle. Oberg was annoyed that the *Arkadia* gang had been hauled in at such an ungodly hour. It had interrupted the orgy with the yawning mistress who sat on the edge of his desk.

His cold eyes took them in one by one. He stopped at Ben Masterton. "You again, Masterton?"

"Just can't stay away from home, Colonel."

"Quiet! No buffoonery," Oberg snapped. He turned

to the clerk at the small desk near his own. "Charge Masterton with espionage and sabotage."

" 'ere we go again . . ."

"Lock him up."

Four massive Nazis surrounded Masterton and marched him off. "See you later, matey," he called. "Remember, they're all bluff. . . ."

The heavy door banged shut after Ben.

The room became quiet.

Oberg slapped his riding crop into an open palm and rocked back and forth in his swivel chair. "I hear we have a Jew here. Step forward, Jew."

No movement from the four.

"Step forward, Jew, I say!"

Yichiel released Elpis and moved to the desk. Oberg continued rocking in his chair.

"What is your name, Jew?"

"I am a British soldier."

The rocking stopped. Oberg arose slowly and walked around the desk. He faced Yichiel. The Palestinian returned his cold Prussian stare. He lifted the riding crop under the boy's nose.

"Your name, Jew?"

"I am a British soldier!"

Oberg raised his arm and slashed the riding crop across Yichiel's cheek. A streak of blood spurted down his face.

He spit in Oberg's face.

In an instant a half dozen brownshirts engulfed him under flailing clubs. They smashed him to the stone floor. He rolled over and held his arms over his face as they kicked.

Elpis' screams tore through him. She knelt beside him and held his head.

"Take him away," Oberg commanded.

The brownshirts dragged a screaming, kicking, clawing Elpis from her husband. Yichiel crawled to his feet and staggered for the door.

"My, my, aren't you the little animal," the Colonel said to Elpis. "Take her to my quarters. Let us see if you make love with such wonderful violence."

Yichiel rushed across the room. A club cracked on his skull. He slumped unconscious to the floor.

Both of them were removed—Elpis still clawing and fighting her three guards.

"She should be delightful—delightful."

His mistress looked bored.

The Prussian returned to his chair and resumed his rocking. He pointed the riding crop at Antonis. "Now don't tell me you are a British soldier, too?"

Antonis stepped forward and answered that he was Antonis, captain of the *Arkadia*.

"Book him, espionage and sabotage."

Mike now stood alone in the center of the room.

The Colonel leaned over to the clerk. "What do we have on this fellow?"

"False travel card, pistol, a million drachmas—no previous record here."

"Your name?"

"Jay Linden."

"We would like to know more about you, Mr. Linden."

"Jay Linden, Lance Corporal, number 359195, New Zealand."

"Go on."

"As a prisoner of war, that is all I am obliged to give."

Oberg's face cracked into a half-smile. He laughed softly. "Very well recited, Lance Corporal Linden."

Mike looked around the room. The brutal brown-shirts awaited a signal. He gritted his teeth and gulped.

Oberg stared through the monocle. Then he resumed his rocking and slapping the riding crop in his palm. "Are you certain you have no more to say, Lance Corporal Linden?"

Mike did not answer.

"You wouldn't be holding some information, Lance Corporal Linden?"

Mike could hear the big clock ticking on the wall. It echoed through the stone room. . . .

Oberg looked up at the clock. He glanced toward the door through which Elpis was taken. "Book him. Sabotage and espionage." Oberg arose and the brownshirts came to attention. He motioned to his clerk. "Get this information on the *Arkadia* over to Gestapo in the morning." He nodded to Mike. "I'm sure Gestapo will make you more anxious to talk." Oberg turned to his mistress. "You may go home," he said. "I shall not want you tonight."

The woman yawned.

Mike was thrown into a black cell. He crawled to his feet and groped about blindly. "Ben," he called. "Ben."

"Over here, matey."

Mike stumbled over sleeping bodies in the dark. The stench of the place was terrific. He made out Ben's immense form kneeling over the prostrate body of Yichiel.

"They gave him a pretty good working over," Ben said.

Yichiel groaned and rolled over.

"They took his wife away. . . . Oberg . . ."

"The bloody bastard! And when he finishes with her he'll turn her over to his guards. . . ."

Mike slipped down to a sitting position on the icy stone floor. He did something he had not done since his childhood. Michael Morrison cried openly and unashamed.

Ben's hand patted his back. "It will be all right, cobber. They won't keep us 'ere long. In about a week we'll be processed and sent to the P.O.W. side of the jail. It's a lot better over on that side. . . ."

Mike pulled himself together and wiped his eyes on his sleeve.

"They'll run us down to Field Police—Gestapo— and they'll question us and charge us with everything, includin' startin' the war. But they're just bluff, all bluff. Just stand up to them and demand your rights as a British soldier and they'll send you to the P.O.W. side. . . ."

"Who—who does the questioning at Gestapo?"

"Oh, he's a mean bugger, chap named Heilser. But don't worry none, Jay—he's all bluff."

FOUR

> *"Out of the night that covers me,*
> *Out of the Pit from pole to pole,*
> *I thank whatever gods may be,*
> *For my unconquerable soul!"*

"Quiet in there, *schweinhund!* Quiet in there, or I kill you. . . ."

> *"Under the bludgeonings of chance,*
> *My head is bloody, but unbowed."*

Ben finished his song, ignoring the crazed head guard, a sadistic Austrian named Hans, who continued to rave outside the cell.

"Beautiful song, ain't it, Jay?" Ben said. "You know, Jay, can't say as I like the 'ospitality 'ere."

Ben had managed to calm Mike considerably. His example of courage, of defiance in the face of the brutal guards was a tonic. And some of Mike's fear had vanished in the two days in Averof. He knew that hell could be no worse for he had now seen the cesspool of humanity.

Their cell couldn't have held forty men properly. It contained ninety "Greek saboteurs." There were no bunks, no heat, no toilet facilities, no water. Only stone and bars. The other "saboteurs" ranged from a boy of ten who had stolen a carton of cigarettes to a man of eighty who had stolen a loaf of bread. Several of the inmates were in a stage of babbling idiocy and there were a dozen obvious T.B. cases ... Lice swarmed everywhere. Mammoth rats roamed.

At night the stone turned icy and the only warmth became the heat of the tightly packed bodies. Their daily meal was a slimy bean soup, without beans. Ben told Mike he would learn to love the stuff and Ben taught Mike how to filch potato peels and garbage from the galley during the visits to the toilet. Ben, an old hand at Averof, immediately found a guard who would pass notes to the outside and who would smuggle in food. Money talked in Averof. The inmate with connections could manage to survive.

Each morning dead men were pulled from the tank.

From one of the two small windows Mike could look

down into the center courtyard of Averof. Twenty-four hours a day horrible torture sessions went on. Each dawn a firing squad eliminated another batch of "saboteurs"—men who stood shivering against the gray stone wall. Each dawn the guard Hans would select some "saboteur" from Mike's tank for execution. He would line up all the prisoners in the corridor and taunt them as he limped up and down the line, an insane smirk on his face.

On the fourth morning, Elpis was dragged to the stone wall in the courtyard. Her screams were feeble but they still reached her husband's ears. The girl was beyond recognition. They strapped her to a post. And as the firing squad lined up, Hans, in the corridor outside the cell, screamed taunts at Yichiel. He boasted that he had been one of the fifty guards who had raped her the night before.

Ben and Mike kept a suicide watch over the bereaved Palestinian.

Four days passed. Michael Morrison was no longer afraid. A seething, boiling anger inside him would not let him be still. But each day brought him closer to the moment when he must come face to face with Konrad Heilser. His mind worked desperately on a plan to avoid the meeting. Perhaps he would feign sickness—perhaps he would try to make a break enroute to Gestapo headquarters—perhaps he would take a crack at Hans and be thrown into solitary . . .

A thousand ideas passed through his mind. All of them except one seemed hopeless.

The one slim hope was Ben's connection with the outside world—a Greek guard named Axiotis. He was one of the very few in Averof inherited by the Germans. The ancient jailer ran a profitable business of smuggling out messages and smuggling in bread, wine and tobacco. Hans was aware of it, but allowed it to continue as long as he received a portion of Axiotis' take.

Ben knew a dozen women on the outside who kept him and Mike and Yichiel in food and tobacco. Mike kept close watch, waiting for Axiotis to pull a doublecross, but the old jailer delivered every time Ben sent him on a mission.

But whom could Mike contact? He did not know where to reach Lisa, and there was the remote possibility that Lisa had been mixed up in his capture. He tried to drive the thought from his mind but it persisted.

Contact Chesney? No. Mike was certain that Chesney had played out a game to lull him into security and staged the capture with such adroitness as to remove any taint of suspicion from himself. After all, Antonis had not showed the least concern. He had acted almost as if he expected to be picked up by the patrol boat. And where was Antonis now? All new prisoners came through Hans' cell block, and he had not seen Antonis. Most likely Antonis was preparing another batch of British soldiers for capture.

Ben insisted on taking the blame, certain that in his drunkenness the night before sailing he had spilled to someone. But Mike could not be sure of that.

Contact Dr. Thackery? He couldn't. Lisa had said that Thackery had been forced into hiding. Even so, the American Archaeological Society was certain to be under the scrutiny of the Gestapo.

One thread remained. It was as fragile as the rest, but he'd have to try it.

Each day brought him closer to Konrad Heilser. Ben looked forward to it for it meant transfer to the P.O.W. side of Averof.

On the fifth day Yichiel was removed from the cell.
The sixth day passed.

"Have you ever been across the sea to Ireland?"
Ben Masterton had resorted to singing Irish ballads.
"Quiet in there!"
"When maybe at the closin' of the day . . ."
"Schweinhund!"
*"You can sit and watch the sun come over Claddock
. . ."*
"I'll kill you if you don't quiet down!"
"Trouble with Hans, Jay, he's got no soul for culture
. . . And watch the barefoot gosels at their play."
Hans stopped his raving suddenly. Ben's voice con-
tinued bellowing. . . .
*"If there's ever to be a life hereafter, and faith, now,
sure I know there's going to be . . ."*
At the end of the corridor, Colonel Oberg and his
staff were marching along crisply, inspecting the cages
of misery. His bored mistress was at his side. Ben raced
up to the bars.
"Hey, wienerschnitzel!"
Oberg whirled about.
"Hey, why don't you be a good bloke and send us
over to the other side of the yard with the P.O.W.'s?"
"Aha, my two British saboteurs."
"Now, come on, wienerschnitzel. In another two
days we'll be as nutty as your guards."
"I take it, Herr Masterton, you've had enough of
Greek criminals?"
"I've had enough of you savin' the world from com-
munism. I just don't like the 'ospitality 'ere."
For some curious reason, Colonel Oberg seemed to

feel some affection for Ben Masterton. A smile cracked his Prussian lips.

"And while you're about it," Ben said, "I'd like to know what 'appened to our cobber?"

"The Jew?"

"The British soldier."

"Rather unfortunate, Ben. He took ill—quite ill ..."

"I'll bet he did!"

Oberg looked angry at first, then sighed in disgust. He turned to his clerk. "See that Herr Masterton and his friend are taken to Gestapo tomorrow and sent over to the P.O.W. compound on return."

"Thanks, matey."

"Masterton, do me a favor. The next time you escape—please don't get recaptured."

"But, Jay," Ben said, "you don't have to pay Axiotis no hundred thousand drachmas to just take out one simple little note for you."

"Look, stop asking questions, Ben. I've got to get it out tonight."

Ben shrugged. "But a hundred thousand drachmas ..."

Axiotis nodded. A grin broke out on the ancient jailer's face as he pocketed the money. He was told that a return message would bring another hundred thousand. The note was addressed to Lazarus, a truck farmer in Chalandri with instructions to get the message to Lisa immediately.

It read:

Helena: I am in Averof. Tomorrow I am to be taken to Gestapo for questioning. Vassili.

FIVE

Heilser's face tightened as he crumpled the message. He was in serious trouble now. Von Ribbentrop had certainly selected the worst possible time for a visit to Greece. British escapees were roaming all over the country and resistance was increasing daily. Just how many documents had already been stolen from the Germans would be known when and if Morrison made his escape and contacted the British. Konrad Heilser sat on a powder keg and the fuse grew short.

He gulped a sedative and rubbed his throbbing temples. The old self-assurance was shattered now. If only he could lay hands on Morrison and learn the names on the Stergiou list, it would throw the entire Underground into a panic. He sank into a chair behind his marble-top desk and mixed another sedative.

Zervos entered without knocking. He smiled at his squirming confederate. No matter who took over the Gestapo, he, Zervos, was secure in his position.

"Konrad," Zervos said, "it is time for our appointment with Lisa."

Heilser thumbed through the papers on his desk. "You go. Colonel Oberg phoned this morning from Averof. He is sending two British escapees over for questioning."

"Oh? Anyone of importance?"

"Only that nuisance, Ben Masterton. I wish he'd make one of his escapes good."

"The other?"

Heilser looked at the preliminary report. "New Zealander, name of Linden—Jay Linden. First time. We have no records on him."

Zervos smirked. "I'll give your regards to Lisa." He turned toward the door.

"Wait. Inform Lisa she is to meet me at my suite at the Grande Bretagne tonight at eight o'clock."

"It won't do you any . . ."

"Do as I say!"

"Very well, Konrad."

Heilser went to the couch, stretched out and rubbed his temples. How his head ached! How it ached!

"Masterton! Linden! Come with us!"

Several guards surrounded the two men as they stepped from the cell. Mike's and Ben's wrists were handcuffed behind them.

They were marched down a long corridor, the sound of the guards' heels resounding hollowly.

After a series of locked doors they emerged in the courtyard of the prison.

Two black cars were waiting.

"You, Linden, in the first auto!"

Mike sat between a pair of plainclothes Gestapo men. An armed soldier sat in the front seat alongside the driver.

The doors shut. The car moved slowly through the courtyard. The mammoth gates of Averof Prison opened. The cars rolled out, turned on their sirens and raced for the center of Athens and German Field Police Headquarters.

Near Concord Square they were forced to slow down.

Mike was thrown from his seat as the driver slammed on his brakes. A truck bolted over the inter-section of Patission and Chalkokondili Streets and stopped directly in their path.

The driver leaned on his horn.

It all happened in seconds.

Two dozen armed Greeks swarmed from the truck and surrounded the two cars. The drivers and guards were dragged out, disarmed and forced to lay on their faces on the sidewalk.

"Morrison! This way!"

Michalis, a tommy gun cradled in his arm, pulled Mike from the car and pulled him along up the street. A car waited at the corner. Michalis pushed Mike into it.

Ben Masterton ran toward the crowd around Concord Square. "See you in Berlin, matey!" he yelled to Mike.

Mike looked back from his car as it ripped into motion. He saw the German autos being turned over in the street and the armed Greeks pouring back into the truck which headed in the opposite direction.

"Hurry! Dammit! Hurry!" Michalis roared at the driver in the voice that could be heard clear up to Salonika.

The phone rang.

Heilser staggered from the couch, groggy from the sedatives. He shook his head and lifted the receiver. "Yes?"

"Konrad, this is Zervos. I am at Anton's Dress Shop."

"What is it?"

"Lisa did not keep her appointment."

"What!"

"I said, Lisa did not come today."

"Why?"

"How should I know?"

"Get back here! Immediately!"

"Very well ..."

Heilser could not understand what that meant. He walked to the basin and ducked his head under the coldwater tap. It cleared a little. He wiped his face and lit a cigarette and meditated.

A knock on the door. The brown-shirted orderly stepped in.

"Manolis Kyriakides to see you, sir."

Heilser frowned. Lisa's husband? What the devil! Maybe he knew ...

"Send him in."

"Yes, sir."

Manolis Kyriakides was ushered in. At one time he might have been a handsome man, but now his eyes were shifty and frightened. He might once have stood tall and straight, but now he cringed in the attitude of a coward. Beads of sweat trickled down his nose and chin as he stood in front of Heilser with his hat in his hand.

"Well!"

"Herr ... Herr ..."

"What is it? Where is your wife?"

"The—the children—they—have been kidnapped!"

Heilser leaped to his feet and grabbed Manolis by the collar and shook him so violently the drops of sweat bounced from his face. Heilser backed him across the room and threw him into a chair.

Manolis trembled.

"Speak!"

"Water, please ..."

"Speak, I say!"

He emitted a feeble croak from his cracked lips. "They came last night. ... Lisa—let them, a dozen men—shot the guards, took the children." Manolis closed his eyes and wept.

"Last night!" Heilser screamed. "Why weren't we informed immediately?"

"They—they—said they'd kill me if I came to you before . . ."

Heilser smashed Manolis' face over and over. Manolis fell to the floor sobbing hysterically.

"Guards! Guards! Take him to Averof!"

Heilser sat at his desk pounding the marble top. Collaborators! Why do we have to have collaborators to win a war? Why do we have to cultivate them, coddle them, bribe them? Men like Zervos and Manolis Kyriakides . . .

Why don't we have men like Ioannis Rodites and Stergiou serving us! Why not men like the mysterious priest, Papa-Panos and the fierce Michalis and the incredibly courageous Thanassis?

Why am I always surrounded with the dregs of humanity?

The door opened.

Zervos stepped in. "Konrad," he said, "brace yourself. Morrison was in Averof. He has escaped."

SIX

The wine cellar beneath Gyni's Restaurant on Armodiou Place was pitch black. Mike and Lisa huddled in a corner. He drew her close and stroked her hair.

"They should come soon," she said.

"It will be all right, honey," he whispered. "It will be all right."

Mike recounted the afternoon's events. Enroute to Gestapo Headquarters, Michalis had led a daring ambush in downtown Athens. In only a matter of minutes he had been transferred to three different cars, the last taking him to this temporary sanctuary.

She told him everything. Papa-Panos had convinced Michalis, Thanassis and Dr. Thackery to let Lisa remain alive in the hope that Morrison would contact her in the event of trouble. Papa-Panos was proven right. Axiotis, the aged jailer at Averof, had delivered the note to Lazarus in Chalandri. In an hour the message was in Lisa's hands.

Then Lisa pulled her coup. Before she would turn over the information to Thanassis and Michalis, she demanded the freedom of her children as ransom for the information on Mike's whereabouts. Within another hour the raid on Manolis' home was over and the children were hidden in the pump house in Chalandri.

Mike looked up at the faces of three angry men in the cellar of Gyni's. They were furious with him because he had permitted emotions to complicate his grave situation. They lashed out at him for forcing them to risk the daylight ambush on the Gestapo. At this point they demanded he turn over the Stergiou list, insisting that he had bungled long enough.

Mike refused, unless Lisa and her sons were permitted to leave Greece with him.

Michalis, Thanassis and Dr. Thackery were faced with the choice of executing both of them and losing the Stergiou list or getting the four of them out of Greece. An impossible task . . .

The trapdoor opened. The beam of a flashlight pierced the darkness of the wine cellar.

Mike could make out the stocky form of Michalis and the long thin form of Dr. Thackery as they threaded their way through the rows of wine kegs.

Mike pressed Lisa's hand. . . .

The flashlight found them. The two men stood over them.

"Very well, Morrison," Dr. Thackery said. "A British submarine will pick you up within forty-eight hours."

"The children?" Lisa asked.

"They are safe. They will join you once we get you clear of Athens," Michalis said.

"If we get clear of Athens," Dr. Thackery added. "Heilser has the city closed tighter than a drum. Nothing can get through the blockade. You have only a fifty-fifty chance, Morrison. You also have forty-eight hours to reconsider turning the list over to us. We will hide you and Lisa in the hills. . . ."

"Not on your life, Dr. Thackery."

"All right—we try for the submarine. I hope we can clear you out of Athens."

"Wait a minute," Mike said. "Wait a minute. I may possibly have an idea . . ."

Julius Chesney drummed his fingers slowly on the table. He looked at Thanassis dubiously.

"This is risky, very risky . . ."

"It is risky for me too," Thanassis said.

"I'll have to think about it," Chesney wheezed.

"Yes or no. They are due to leave within forty-eight hours."

"You make it very difficult, dear fellow. If it wasn't for the money . . ."

"That's why I came to you with this proposition. I've heard of your love for drachmas."

Julius Chesney's jowls quivered as he emitted his nasty little laugh. "Agreed," he said.

"And half of what you collect from the Germans belongs to me," Thanassis said.

"Agreed," Chesney nodded, "agreed."

"Here is the information to date, then. Morrison and Lisa Kyriakides are now in Athens. I do not know where, inasmuch as I have not seen Michalis since he made the ambush. A British submarine will be here to get them sometime within forty-eight hours."

Chesney nodded.

Thanassis continued. "I will give you their route from Athens and contact point with the submarine just as soon as I learn it."

"Just how do your people expect to get them out of Athens?"

"That is the problem, Mr. Chesney. I will not know until I see Dr. Thackery or Michalis."

Chesney thought of the drachmas and laughed again. He extended his fat hand over the table. Thanassis eyed him with suspicion for a moment, then shook his hand.

Thanassis arose. "Remember," he said, "half the money is mine."

"Tell me, Professor Thanassis, just why are you doing this?"

"Because they don't have a chance."

"Do find your own way to the door," Chesney wheezed. He was clearly wedged into his seat. "Bad heart, dear fellow—bad heart."

Chesney's slitted eyes followed Thanassis as the scholarly appearing man turned and walked from the room.

Chesney struggled to his feet and waddled to the

phone, searched out a number and dialed with a pencil, unable to fit his finger into the dial holes.

"Hello . . ."

"Hello, Konrad?"

"Yes."

"This is Chesney, Julius Chesney."

"What is it?"

"Could you and Zervos come up to my place right away?"

"At this hour of the morning, Julius?"

"It concerns a mutual friend of ours. An American chap, I believe. . . ."

"I'll be right over."

"Yes . . . And Konrad, dear fellow, do bring your check book with you."

Chesney studied the harassed face of Konrad Heilser. Usually the German was a picture of complacency but now he was tense and drawn and snappy. Zervos, the diamond display case, sat beside him.

"Drink?"

"Scotch, double," Heilser said.

Zervos agreed to the same.

Chesney waddled to the bar.

"Now then, Konrad. What I am about to say is of great interest to you. . . ."

"Get to the point. If you know something about Morrison, how much do you want?"

"You are getting ahead of yourself, Konrad. Very well. I am about to fall heir to complete information on his whereabouts. I want fifty million drachmas for the information—not a drachma less."

"Fifty million! Are you insane?"

"Don't tempt me, dear fellow. I'm liable to ask for the Acropolis too."

"Fifty million is out of the question."

"Then, gentlemen, let me say it is beyond my bedtime. I believe you know your way to the door?"

Heilser fumed. Again he was in the clutches of the dregs of humanity. Fifty million would wipe out the personal fortune he had worked so hard to gather in Greece. He thought quickly. He'd force half the amount from Zervos—and he'd see to it that Chesney never left Greece alive. He looked at Zervos. The fat man shrugged.

"He drives a hard bargain, Konrad. We have little choice."

"Very well," Heilser muttered. "Where is he?"

Chesney held up his fat palm. "Ahhhh, not so fast, not so fast. You will cable the money to my bank in Argentina. As soon as I receive confirmation of the deposit . . ."

"You swine!"

Chesney laughed and cracked his knuckles and reached for the platter of olives on the table. "I may add, dear fellow, that you must move rather quickly. A British submarine will pick him up within forty-eight hours. And, Konrad, as an extra little bonus, I will also deliver Lisa Kyriakides and her children at no extra charge to you."

The German snatched his hat from the table. "You will receive confirmation of the deposit by tomorrow, noon."

They started to leave but Zervos was puzzled about something. "Just why do you want your money in Argentina?" he asked.

"It is like this, Mr. Zervos. I don't trust you. I trust Herr Heilser, but I don't trust you. And it is my very candid opinion as a learned correspondent that Germany is going to lose this war."

He popped an olive into his mouth.

SEVEN

Papa-Panos held a flickering candle. Lisa, Mike, Dr. Thackery and Michalis stood in a tight circle. Thanassis stood a few paces behind them, leaning on a wine keg.

"Set your watches, everyone. It is now exactly twelve, noon," Dr. Thackery said.

They strained their eyes in the poor light.

"Today it will be dark at ten minutes past seven," Dr. Thackery continued. "At seven-thirty we begin to make the move from Athens. By eight-fifteen we should reach Chalandri and pick up your two boys, Lisa."

She nodded.

"From Chalandri we dash for the coast. We will be traveling on secondary roads and it will not be too fast." He unfolded a map and placed it on the cement floor. Everyone knelt over it. Thanassis moved from the wine keg and bent over Lisa's shoulder. Dr. Thackery's pencil traced a line. "At this point along the Gulf we will have to take off by foot. You will be met by a man—he will take you to the rendezvous cove. The man's name is Meletis. Now, after you reach the Gulf it will be over an hour's hike. You reach the Gulf no later than ten-thirty."

Dr. Thackery drew an X on the map. "This is rendezvous point. Sheltered cove here—quite isolated. A sentry will be on the hill behind you with a beacon light. A few minutes before midnight he will blink three times to the submarine. This signal will be repeated every five minutes until the submarine surfaces and returns the signal. A party will row ashore in rubber boats and take you aboard. Is that all clear?"

Everyone nodded.

"Where are you going now, Thanassis?" Michalis asked.

"I must go out for a while," he replied.

"Are all your arrangements completed?"

"All my arrangements are quite completed," Thanassis answered. He turned on his flashlight and made his way through the cellar to the ladder and disappeared through the trapdoor.

"He acts rather odd, sometimes," Dr. Thackery observed. "I wonder if he is getting nervous?"

"We are all nervous," Mike said.

Dr. Thackery folded the map and stood up. Papa-Panos blew out the candle and plunged the place into darkness. Lisa leaned against Mike and closed her eyes.

"It's all right, honey, it will be over soon. . . ."

"I still don't like his choice of getting out of Athens," Michalis said.

"It is our only chance, Michalis," Dr. Thackery said. "We must make the move. It will be only a matter of time until someone goes to the Gestapo."

Thanassis had lost much of his scholarly calm.

"You told me that my share would be twenty million drachmas!"

"*Dear* fellow," Julius Chesney wailed, dramatizing their mutual plight. "Twenty million was all I could get from Heilser. We agreed to split, fifty-fifty. This is your share, ten million."

Thanassis counted the ten million drachmas. He was gone beyond return with Chesney and, although he knew he was being cheated, he had no choice now. It was a cheat's game. He placed the money in his pocket. "Very well. You have all the details."

Chesney nodded.

"I will see you at the cove at midnight, then."

"Ah, Konrad and Zervos. Right on time, I see."

"The information," Heilser snapped. "Do you have it?"

"Yes, I have it. And I do thank you for the prompt transfer of fifty million to my bank. Drink, gentlemen?"

Heilser was already at the bar and poured himself a half tumbler of Scotch. His hand trembled. He emptied half the glass in one gulp, some of the Scotch dribbling down his chin.

Julius Chesney unfolded a map of the province of Attica-Boeotia and placed it on the bar.

"Morrison and Lisa are departing from Athens at seven-thirty tonight."

"Where are they?"

"Apparently they are changing hideouts every hour, so no one is absolutely certain."

Heilser took another swig of Scotch.

Julius Chesney continued. "It also seems they have mapped a half dozen alternate ways of leaving Athens, so I cannot give you specifics on that, either."

"Go on. . ."

"What I do know is this: A submarine will contact them at this point. Now, gentlemen. They leave Athens at seven-thirty. At eight-fifteen they are to rendezvous with Lisa's sons who are hiding somewhere on the outskirts. From there they dash by car to Marathon." Chesney's pencil drew a line past the town of Nea Makri and farther north past Soros. His pencil stopped at a heavily forested area on the coast. "There is a cove at this point. They are due to arrive at the cove five minutes before midnight using an approach from the south."

Heilser studied the map for several moments. He turned to Zervos. "Do you know this area?"

"Yes. It is perfect—well chosen for a submarine. Quite isolated—many coves, smooth sea, good cover with a forest in the background and no towns or troops for miles."

"At midnight," Chesney said, "a sentry will be on this hill above the cove. He will signal for the submarine to surface."

Heilser was on his feet pacing the room. "We must triple the guard around Athens. I will move a battalion of men along the escape route. Another company will cover the rendezvous point. . . ."

"Just a minute, dear fellow, just a minute," Chesney halted Heilser. "You paid fifty million drachmas for this information. I would truly be embarrassed if you did not come up with Mr. Morrison."

"Exactly what do you mean?"

"First off, you are underestimating your opposition. They have men posted observing all of your roadblocks out of Athens. They also have a man going in advance of their main party to make sure the route is clear. At the first indication of trouble they are either going to use an alternate or return to hiding. The moment you blanket the area with troops they'll call it off."

"He makes good sense, Konrad," Zervos said.

"We cannot for a moment arouse their suspicions by throwing out a general alarm. You know as well as I do that Morrison could hide inside Athens for fifteen years and you'd never find him. Also, if he is forced into hiding again the Stergiou list may be passed to the British by any one of a hundred people. Thus far, Morrison has refused to give it up."

The German was annoyed with himself. Yes, he'd certainly bungle things if he tried to use five thousand troops. A sudden movement of soldiers was certain to send Morrison into hiding again and Chesney was right when he said that there was little hope of finding him inside Athens.

"All right. What do you suggest?"

"I suggest that you leave Athens immediately and try to get north of Marathon. That way you could come in from the south and avoid their route and avoid their lookouts. You can slip into the rendezvous area at dark with, say, twenty or thirty heavily armed men and await their arrival."

Heilser again studied the map and pondered. He looked to Zervos and Zervos nodded in agreement.

"Very well. We leave Athens right away. Zervos, get the road-blocks lifted around the city and pick thirty of our best men. We meet in an hour and drive north of Marathon and wait till dark. Then we move to the cove."

"Now you talk sense," Chesney said.

"One more thing," Heilser added.

"Yes?"

"You are going with us, Mr. Chesney."

"By all means, dear fellow, by all means. I wouldn't miss this for the world."

EIGHT

Six o'clock.

Lisa was terribly shaken by the news. "I knew he was not a good man, but he was my husband," she whispered. "Somehow, I feel that I should have helped him. Years ago, I could have helped him. He was sick—sick with ambition."

"Don't blame yourself, darling."

"Manolis—dead—shot by the Germans in Averof. Will it never end, Michael? Will it never end?"

The time ticked on ruthlessly.

Six-thirty.

"You'll love San Francisco, Lisa."

"Hold me, Michael, hold me—I'm frightened."

"We'll get through, darling, we'll get through."

Six forty-five.

"It is beginning to turn dark outside," Papa-Panos said. "They will be here in a few minutes."

"*Panagia, Panagia,*" Lisa whispered with her eyes closed. "*Panagia* . . . Holy Mother . . ."

The minutes ticked on.

Seven o'clock.

Mike, taut with nerves, tried to find calm in his pipe. He checked his pistol. Lisa checked hers.

The trapdoor opened. Dr. Thackery made his way down the ladder. His flashlight picked them out in the darkness.

"Everything is ready," he said.

"Where is Thanassis?"

"He has gone in advance."

"Does the route look clear?"

"Almost too clear—almost too clear . . ."

"Papa-Panos," Lisa said, "Would you pray with me?"

"Yes, my child."

Seven-fifteen.

The four of them stood in utter silence. Above they could hear the creak of footsteps on the floor as the evening meal began in Gyni's Restaurant. They could hear each other breathe. . . .

Seven twenty-five.

The trapdoor opened.

Michalis came down the ladder. "The car is waiting," he said.

Mike drew a deep breath and squeezed Lisa's hand.

"God be with you," Papa-Panos said.

"Let us be gone," Michalis urged.

"Just a moment," Dr. Thackery said. He handed some small capsules to Lisa and Mike.

"If anything goes wrong, you are to swallow these."

"What is it?"

"Cyanide."

Marathon was quiet in the moonlight. There was a sandy cove and a sheer wall above it. A rocky path led down to the beach. On the rim of the wall there was a growth of tall grass and brush and beyond that a forest rising to a high hill.

The hour was eleven o'clock.

Julius Chesney and Zervos, the two fat men, were hardest hit by the grueling walk through the forest.

The officer reported to Heilser for instructions.

"Spread your men along the rim, overlooking the cove," Heilser whispered. "I want absolutely no movement until you clear with me."

The captain nodded and crept off. He whispered commands, dispersing his men behind rocks, in the tall grass and in the brush. They formed a ring around and above the cove. The soldiers held their weapons at the ready. . . .

Heisler, Zervos and Chesney moved up the hill a little to gain a better vantage point of the entire area.

"The men moved in well," Chesney whispered. "I'm positive they were not detected." He pointed his fat finger toward the southern end of the cove. "They should be coming through there. We had better just relax. There is still an hour to wait."

The car stopped off the dirt road. A man ran toward it.

"Where are they?" the man asked the driver.

"The two boys are covered on the rear floor. The man and woman are in the trunk," Ketty, the prostitute, answered.

The man snapped the trunk lid open and assisted Mike and Lisa out. They both reeled dizzily. Ketty uncovered the boys and they ran to their mother.

"I am Meletis," the man said. "I am to take you to the rendezvous."

Mike and Lisa grasped his hands. "Are you all right?"

"Yes, we will be in a minute—soon's we get some air." Mike went to Ketty. "I'll always be in your debt," he said.

"Anything for the Englezos," Ketty answered. "I'm glad you came to me for help."

"Come," Meletis snapped. "We have an hour's walk and there is no time for farewells. Did you have trouble along the route?"

"There was but one challenge," Ketty said. "But I have a very convenient pass signed by Herr Heilser, himself."

"Good-bye, Ketty."

"Good-bye, my Englezos soldier."

"We'll be coming back to Greece some day—with an army that won't be thrown out." He kissed her cheek and ran to catch up with Meletis, Lisa and the boys.

They moved up the coastline.

Five minutes before midnight.

The German captain signaled to his men and back to Heilser. Everything was in order. All eyes were on the southern end of the cove. All one could hear was the gentle lap of the sea against the shore and the rustle of the leaves around them.

"Where are they?"

"Any moment now . . ."

A minute ticked off—two—three . . .

Chesney nudged Heilser and pointed toward the top of the hill behind them. A light shot out toward the water. It went on and off three times. Heilser's heart thudded.

"That is the signal," Chesney said. He squinted nearsightedly at his wristwatch as the seconds ticked off. "At the next signal, everything will be ready."

A soft stir of movement was heard from the forest behind them.

"They are coming," Chesney whispered.

He kept looking at his watch for a full five minutes then glanced up to the hilltop again. The signal light went on and off three more times.

Julius Chesney grunted as he got to his feet and stretched. "Well, Konrad, the game is over," he said.

Heilser looked up at him, too stunned to speak.

"Forgive me, dear fellow. There *is* a submarine, but I failed to mention that it is on the opposite coast of Greece, a hundred kilometers from this point. If my calculations are correct, Lisa and Mr. Morrison should be boarding it at this very minute."

"Seize him!" Heilser shrieked. "Seize him!"

"Oh, no, dear fellow. That signal from the hill was for the purpose of moving two hundred gentlemen into position through the forest. Guerrillas, I believe you call them. The second signal indicated that they have your force surrounded."

The officer came dashing up.

"Herr Heilser, we are surrounded!"

"Order your men to drop their arms, Captain. Resistance is quite useless. You see, I do not wish to die as a Greek martyr and one utterance from me and a mutual friend, Professor Thanassis, will lay down a most dreadful barrage."

Heilser got to his feet. He looked about him. Spread all over the hill, in the brush and behind trees he could see the rifles of the Greek guerrillas. He looked into the empty cove. His face was white, his lips drained of blood. . . .

"Surrender your force," he croaked to his officer. He turned to Chesney. "You'll never get away with this."

"Oh, I don't know about that. By the time they find your body—provided they do find your body—I shall be enjoying a good gin and tonic in the Press Club in London. You see, Konrad, at my request you went to great lengths to keep your move a secret. No one knows just where you are."

Zervos scrambled to his feet. His eyes bulged like a madman's. "Julius," he blubbered, "Julius—I am wealthy. Fifty—a hundred million drachmas—two hundred million—please! Please!" He fell to his knees and kissed Chesney's hand. . . .

A shot cracked out.

Zervos clutched his stomach and rolled over, dead. Konrad Heilser handed his pistol to Chesney.

"Collaborators," Heilser snarled. "I have no use for a man who would sell out his own country. I underestimated you, Julius. I should have known that, devil that you are, you would not have turned traitor."

"Dear me," Chesney said, throwing the pistol to the ground, "these things make me extremely nervous."

"I will spare you the dramatics of Zervos. I shall die quite quietly."

"Well, let us not say that I was prompted by patriotic motives. But fortunately there is a bottom to my conscience. You do understand, dear fellow?"

Thanassis walked up to them. "The Germans are all rounded up. We have their arms. Let us get on with it."

"You are going to execute me now?"

"Unfortunately, yes, dear fellow. We have no choice."

Konrad Heilser walked slowly to a large boulder, lit a cigarette and waited. Chesney beckoned Thanassis to wait for a few moments. He walked beside the German. Heilser was calm now—a return to the old Heilser. He had lost the game, his usefulness was gone.

"Tell me, Julius, how did you manage it?"

"Ingenious plan, I must say. You see, the Underground had a very serious problem. To move Lisa and Morrison with secrecy and to get them from Athens. Thanassis came to me with the idea to use myself as a decoy by luring you to the wrong coast and at the same time getting the roadblocks lifted from Athens. You were of great help to the Underground, I must say, Konrad."

"And I also financed the trip. . . ."

Chesney leaned close. "Be a good chap and don't tell Thanassis how much I was paid. I did take a bit more than my share, but I hear Thanassis is going to use his end to buy arms for the Underground."

"We must get going," Thanassis called.

"You know, Konrad, even if you had taken Morrison and even if you discovered the names on the Stergiou list, I wonder, I seriously wonder if it would have made a difference in the end. Oh, yes, the world is filled with bumbling amateurs like Michael Morrison and Lisa Kýriakides. They brush temptation, they are given to sentiment, they wrangle with their consciences— but somehow the Michaels and the Lisas end up on the path of the righteous. I'm afraid, dear fellow, there are too many Michaels and Lisas in this world for scoundrels like you and me to contend with."

"Let us get on with it," Heilser said softly. He crushed out his cigarette. "I am ready."

Dawn.
The submarine surfaced.

Lisa stood on the deck with her two sons at her side. Michael Morrison, American writer of sorts, amateur in the game of international intrigue, stood behind her. He touched her shoulder softly as the coastline of North Africa appeared on the horizon before them.

ABOUT THE AUTHOR

LEON URIS, born in Baltimore in 1924, left high school to join the Marine Corps. In 1950, Esquire magazine bought an article from him—and it encouraged him to begin work on a novel. The result was his acclaimed bestseller *Battle Cry. The Angry Hills*, a novel set in war-time Greece, was his second book. As a screen writer and then newspaper correspondent, he became interested in the dramatic events surrounding the rebirth of the state of Israel. This interest led to *Exodus*, his monumental success which has been read by millions of people. From one of the episodes in *Exodus* came *Mila 18*, the story of the angry uprising of Jewish fighters in the Warsaw Ghetto. *Exodus Revisited*, a work of non-fiction, presents the author's feeling for the land and the people of Israel. And Mr. Uris is also the author of *Armageddon, Topaz,* and his latest, *QB VII*—all sensational bestsellers.

At present, Leon Uris lives in Aspen, Colorado with his wife, Jill.